The Elect Lady.

Fiction From Victor Books.

The Elect Lady

George MacDonald

edited by
Dan Hamilton

VICTOR BOOKS ®
A DIVISION OF SCRIPTURE PRESS PUBLICATIONS INC.
USA CANADA ENGLAND

The Elect Lady was first published in England in 1888.

Library of Congress Catalog Card Number: 87-62496
ISBN: 0-89693-451-9

Cover Illustration: James Fennison

VICTOR BOOKS
A division of Scripture Press Publications, Inc.
Wheaton, Illinois 60187

Contents.

Editor's Foreword.

The Elect Lady first appeared in 1888, when MacDonald was sixty-four years old. It was his twenty-third novel for adults; most of his more important and durable works were behind him. MacDonald was still writing *of* his native Scotland but not now *in* her. For the preservation of their fragile health, he and his family were living in Casa Corragio (House of Courage) in Bordighera, Italy, returning to England and Scotland only in the warmer summer months. In the previous year they had survived the violent Italian earthquake that would later be featured in *A Rough Shaking.**

MacDonald's books had earned him fame and a following, but precious little fortune. He sold outright to his publishers the copyrights to many of his books, and therefore received none of the return of soaring sales. Pirate editions were published—many in the United States—without his permission or involvement, and therefore brought him no financial reward.

He was continually pressed for money, but seldom grumbled over its lack; nevertheless, of his agent he once asked, "How is it that while I have ten times the number of readers I had ten years ago, I cannot get nearly such good prices for my books?"

Though he had little money at any given time, MacDonald was generous with what he had, and always counted himself a blessed man. Casa Corragio was, as his other homes had been, a

---

*A Rough Shaking has been republished by Winner Books as *The Wanderings of Clare Skymer.*

busy center of hospitality and healing, a stage for lectures and plays, and a chapel for worship and instruction.

The Elect Lady was written in such surroundings. It is a fine story, but has been largely neglected by MacDonald's admirers and his critics. It was apparently not written as a magazine serial, and therefore has the unusual property (for a MacDonald novel, at least) of being relatively short and direct in both its narrative and message. My major editing function here has been to rephrase a large number of awkward and rambling sentences, and to translate the broad Scots tongue (beautiful but only partially intelligible to us now) into something we might comprehend with undiminished delight.

This book is more than unusually rich in penetrating, personal asides between "I" the narrator and "you" the reader; I have left most of these passages intact, for they add to the warmth of the story—as if he were telling us a tale by the fireside, a story told to friends he knows well, about friends he knew well once upon a time. And, as odd as they may seem in our time, and given our preferences in style, to recast or eliminate these passages is to destroy their precise beauty.

I have also attempted to illuminate some of MacDonald's literary background where it surfaces in the story. He was an unusually well-read man, and he often quoted from or alluded to books or poetry either not familiar or not readily available to us today. Some of these quotes and allusions and obscure terms are amplified or explained in the special Appendix at the back of this book.

The Elect Lady is a short novel, published at a time when anything less than a three-volume book was not viewed as serious reading. Yet it is important to MacDonald admirers because it is a well-done reiteration of his favorite themes—the nobility which is earned rather than inherited, the folly of any society which perpetuates the very existence of social classes, and the inestimable value of personal holiness and simple obedience to God.

It is also a fair summary of all he questioned and doubted and believed and hoped and practiced. He questioned the true effect and usefulness of the formally established church; the stern and unbending nature of the God portrayed by Scottish Calvinism; and the basic value of any so-called "virtue" praised by the world. He himself led more than a few small "churches" of the kind that gathered naturally around Andrew—groups assembled on the spot with whoever would come. Yet, unlike many other men who have used their gifts wrongly to draw other men to them and away from God, MacDonald used his insight and influence and popularity and magnetism to draw other men *with* him so that they might behold God as he saw Him.

He excelled in depicting the love of God the Father toward His children, and is well worth reading for his insight into the human heart. Yet not all in MacDonald can be commended without reservation. In reacting against the strict stony doctrines of his upbringing, he came to embrace certain aspects of universalism, the belief that all men everywhere would eventually be reconciled to God—and if not in this world, then in the next.

I cannot agree with MacDonald, based on my understanding of the Scriptures, but I certainly sympathize with his longings that God would not suffer any of His created beings to dwell in the outer darkness forever, and that all men would eventually be reconciled to God through Christ, at whatever eventual cost to themselves. Yet MacDonald's concept encompassed not just all men redeemed, but the whole creation as well; I have more confidence in his hope that at least some animals—especially the pets and animal friends we have known and loved—will join us in the life eternal.

Dan Hamilton
Indianapolis, Indiana
August 1987

9

Introduction.

George MacDonald (1824-1905), a Scottish preacher, poet, novelist, fantasist, expositor, and public figure, is most well known today for his children's books—*At the Back of the North Wind, The Princess and the Goblin, The Princess and Curdie*, and his fantasies *Lilith* and *Phantastes*.

But his fame is based on far more than his fantasies. His lifetime output of more than fifty popular books placed him in the same literary realm as Charles Dickens, Wilkie Collins, William Thackeray, and Thomas Carlyle. He numbered among his friends and acquaintances Lewis Carroll, Mark Twain, Lady Byron, and John Ruskin.

Among his later admirers were G.K. Chesterton, W.H. Auden, and C.S. Lewis. MacDonald's fantasy *Phantastes* was a turning point in Lewis' conversion; Lewis acknowledged MacDonald as his spiritual master, and declared that he had never written a book without quoting from MacDonald.

Chapter 1

LANDLORD'S DAUGHTER AND TENANT'S SON

The kitchen of the laird's old stone house was of moderate size, flagged with slate, and humble in its appointments. In the corner, with a white deal table between them, sat two young people—different in rank, and meeting upon no apparent level of friendship.

The young man was easily mistaken as having a weaker nature than the young woman, and the deference he showed her as his superior enhanced the difficulty of making a true judgment. He was tall and thin, but plainly in fine health, with a sunburned complexion. His clear hazel eyes were not large, but were full of light. His mouth was firm, with a curious smile, and now he was unconsciously indulging his habit when perplexed of pinching his upper lip between his finger and thumb. Andrew Ingram was the son of a small farmer, and his companion for the moment was Miss Alexa Fordyce, the daughter of his landlord, the Laird of Potlurg.

The young woman held in her hand a paper which seemed the subject of their conversation. She was about twenty-five, well-grown and not ungraceful, with dark hair, dark hazel eyes, and rather large, handsome features—full of intelligence but a little hard, and not a little proud—as such features must be, except after prolonged influence of a heart potent in self-subjugation. As to her social expression, it was a mingling of the educated gentlewoman and the farmer's daughter, supreme over the household and its share in the labor of production.

"I have glanced over the poem," said the lady, "and it seems to me quite up to the average of what you see in print."

"Would that be reason for printing it, ma'am?" asked the man, with an amused smile.

"It would be for the editor to determine," she answered, not perceiving the hinted objection.

"You will remember, ma'am, that I never suggested—indeed I never thought of such a thing!"

"I do not forget. It was your mother who drew my attention to the verses."

"I must speak to my mother!" he said, in a meditative way.

"You cannot object to *my* seeing your work! She does not show it to everybody. It is most creditable to you, such an employment of your leisure."

"The poem was never meant for any eyes but my own—and my brother's."

"What was the good of writing it, if no one was to see it?"

"The writing of it, ma'am."

"For the exercise, you mean?"

"No, I hardly mean that."

"I am afraid then I do not understand you."

"Do *you* never write anything except to publish it?"

"Publish! *I* never publish! What made you think of such a thing?"

"That you know so much about it, ma'am."

"I know people connected with the papers, and thought it might encourage you to see something in print. The newspapers publish so many poems now!"

"I wish it hadn't been just that one my mother gave you."

"Why?"

"For one thing, it is not finished—as you will see when you read it more carefully."

"I did see a line I thought hardly rhythmical, but—"

"Excuse me, ma'am, but the want of rhythm there was intentional."

"I am sorry for that. Intention is the worst possible excuse for wrong! The accent should always be made to fall in the right place."

"Beyond a doubt; but might not the right place alter with the sense?"

"Never. The rule is strict."

"Is there no danger of making the verse monotonous?"

"Not that I know."

"I have an idea, ma'am, that our great poets owe much of their music to the liberties they take with the rhythm. They treat the rule as its masters, and break it when they see fit."

"You must be wrong there! But in any case you must not presume to take the liberties of a great poet."

"It is a poor reward for being a great poet to be allowed to take liberties. I should say that, doing their work to the best of their power, they were rewarded with the discovery of higher laws of verse. Everyone must walk by the light given him. By the rules which others have laid down, he may learn to walk; but once his heart is awake to truth, and his ear to measure, melody, and harmony, he must walk by the light and the music God gives him."

"That is dangerous doctrine, Andrew!" said the lady, with a superior smile. "But," she continued, "I will mark what faults I see, and point them out to you."

"Thank you, ma'am, but please do not send the verses anywhere."

"I will not except I find them worthy. You need not be afraid! For my father's sake, I will have an eye to your reputation."

"I am obliged to you, ma'am," returned Andrew, but with his curious smile, that had in it a wonderful mixture of sweetness and humor, and something that seemed to sit miles above his amusement. A heavenly smile it was, knowing too much to be angry. It had in it neither offense nor scorn. In respect of his poetry he was shy, but he showed no rejection of the patronage forced upon him by the lady.

He rose and stood a moment.

"Well, Andrew, what is it?"

"When will you allow me to call for the verses?"

"In the course of a week or so. By that time I shall have made up my mind. If in doubt, I shall ask my father."

"I wouldn't like the laird to think I spend much time on poetry."

"You write poetry, Andrew! A man should not do what he would not have known."

"That is true, ma'am. I only feared an erroneous conclusion."

"I will take care of that. My father knows that you are a hardworking young man. There is not one of his farms in better order than yours. Were it otherwise, I should not be so interested in your poetry."

Andrew wished her less interested in it. To have his verses read was like having a finger poked in his eye. He had not known that his mother looked on his papers. But he showed little sign of his annoyance, bade the lady good-morning, and left the kitchen.

Miss Fordyce followed him to the door and stood for a moment looking out. In front of her was a paved court surrounded with low buildings. Between two buildings, at the distance of a mile or so, a railway line was visible where it approached a viaduct. She heard the sound of a coming train, and who in a country place will not stand to see one pass?

Chapter 2.

AN ACCIDENT

While Andrew and Alexa were talking, that same long train was rattling through their dreary country, where it would never have been, were there not regions very different on both sides of it. For miles in any direction, nothing but humpy moorland was to be seen—a gathering of low hills, with now and then a higher one, its sides broken by occasional torrents in poor likeness of a mountain. No smoke proclaimed the presence of human dwelling, but there were spots between the hills where the hand of man had helped a feeble fertility. In front was a small but productive valley, on the edge of which stood the ancient House of Potlurg, with the heath behind it; over a narrow branch of this valley went the viaduct.

It was a slow train, with few passengers. Of these one was looking from his window with a vague sense of superiority, thinking what a forgotten, scarce-created country it seemed. He was a well-dressed, good-looking fellow, with keen but pale gray eyes and a fine forehead, though he had a weak chin. The young man was alone in the first-class carriage of the train. Dressed in a gray suit, he was a little too particular in the smaller points of his attire, and lacked in consequence something of the look of a gentleman. Every now and then he would take off his hard round hat, and pass a white left hand through his short mousy hair, while his right hand caressed his long moustache. A certain indescribable heaviness and lack of light characterized his pale face.

It was a lovely day in early June. The air was rather cold, but youth cares little about temperature on a holiday, with the sun shining, and that sweetest sense of having nothing to do. To many men and women the greatest trouble is to choose, for self is the hardest of masters to please; but as yet George Crawford had not been troubled with much choosing.

With a crowded town behind him, the loneliness he looked upon was a pleasure to him. Compelled to spend time in his own company, without the sense of being on the way out of it, would have soon grown irksome to him; for however much men may be interested *in* themselves, there are few indeed who are interesting *to* themselves. Only those whose self is aware of a higher presence can escape becoming bores and disgusts to themselves. That every man is endlessly greater than what he calls himself, must seem a paradox to the ignorant and dull; but a universe would be impossible without it. George had not arrived at the discovery of this fact, and yet was for the present contented both with himself and with his circumstances.

The heather was not in bloom, and the few flowers of the heathy land made no show. Brown and darker brown predominated, with here and there a shadow of green. Weary of his outlook, George was settling back to his book when there came a great bang and a tearing sound. He started to his feet, and for hours knew nothing more.

The car ahead had run off the line and turned over, and George's carriage had followed it from the viaduct.

Chapter 3.

HELP

"Papa! Papa! There is an accident on the line!" cried Miss Fordyce, running into her father's study, where he sat surrounded with books. "I saw it from the door!"

"Hush!" returned the old man, and listened. "I hear the train going on," he said, after a moment.

"Part of it is come to grief, I am certain," answered his daughter. "I saw something fall from the tracks."

"Well, my dear?"

"What shall we do?"

"What would you have us do?" rejoined her father, without a movement toward rising. "It is too far away for us to be of any use."

"We ought to go and see."

"I am not fond of such seeing, Alexa, and will not go out of my way for it. The misery I cannot avoid is enough for me."

But Alexa was out of the room, and in a moment more was running straight across the heath to the low embankment. Andrew caught sight of her running. Convinced that something was the matter, he turned and ran in the same direction.

It was a hard and long run for Alexa, over such ground. Troubled at her father's indifference, she ran the faster—too fast for thinking, but not too fast for the thoughts that came of themselves. What had come over her father of late? Their house was the nearest! She could not shut out the conviction that, since succeeding to the property, he had been growing less

17

and less neighborly.

She had caught up a bottle of brandy which impeded her running. Yet she made good speed, her dress gathered high in the other hand. With her long dark hair broken loose and flying in the wind, her assumed dignity forgotten, and only the woman within her awake, she ran like a deer over the heather. Though it was a long moor mile, in little more than a quarter of an hour she reached the embankment, flushed and panting.

More than one of the carriages had rolled down, and the rails were a wreck. But the engine and half the train had kept on; neither engineer nor fireman was hurt, and they were hurrying to fetch help from the next station. At the foot of the bank George Crawford lay insensible, with the conductor of the train doing what he could to bring him to consciousness. George was on his back, pale as death, with no motion and scarcely a sign of life.

Alexa tried to give him brandy, but she was so exhausted and her hand shook so that she had to yield the bottle to the conductor. Hale and strong as she was, she could but drag herself a little apart before she fainted.

In the meantime, as the train approached the station, the engineer saw the neighborhood doctor riding nearby, slackened speed, and set his whistle shrieking madly. The doctor set spurs to his horse, and came straight over everything to his side.

"You go on," the doctor said, having heard what had happened. "I shall be there sooner than you could take me."

He came first upon Andrew trying to make Miss Fordyce swallow a little of the brandy.

"There's but one gentleman hurt, sir," said the conductor. "The other's only a young lady that's run till she's dropped."

"To bring brandy," supplemented Andrew.

The doctor recognized Alexa, and wondered what reception her father would give his patient, for to Potlurg he must go! Suddenly she came to herself and sat up, gazing wildly about.

"Out of breath, Miss Fordyce; nothing worse!" said the doctor, as she smiled at him.

He turned to the young man, and did for him what he could without splints or bandages. Then, with the help of the conductor and Andrew, he constructed from pieces of the broken carriages a sort of litter on which to carry him to Potlurg.

"Is he dead?" asked Alexa.

"Not a bit of it. He's had a bad blow on the head, as well as his leg shattered. We must get him somewhere as fast as we can!"

"Do you know him?"

"Not I. But we must take him to your father's house. I don't know what else to do with him."

"What else should you want to do with him?"

"I was afraid it might bother the laird."

"You scarcely know my father, Dr. Pratt!"

"It would be a bother to most people to have a wounded man quartered on them for weeks!" returned the doctor. "Poor fellow! A good-looking one too!"

A country man who had been in the next carriage, but had escaped almost unhurt, offered his service; Andrew and he took up the litter gently, and set out walking with care, the doctor on one side leading his horse, and Miss Fordyce on the other.

It was a strange building to which they eventually drew near, nor did it look the less strange the nearer they came. It was unsheltered by a single tree, and but for a low wall and iron rail on one side, enclosing what had been a garden but was now a grass plot, it rose straight out of the heather. From this plot the ground sloped to the valley, and was under careful cultivation. The entrance to it was closed with a gate of wrought iron, of good workmanship, but so wasted that it seemed on the point of vanishing. Here at one time had been the way to the house, but no door, and scarce a window, was now to be seen on this side of the building. It was very old, and consisted of three gables, a great half-round hall between two of them, and a low tower with a conical roof.

Crawford had begun to recover consciousness; but when he came to himself, he met only acute pain. The least attempt to move was torture, and again he fainted.

Chapter 4.

THE LAIRD

Conducted by the lady, they passed round the house to the court, and across the court to a door in one of the gables. It was a low, narrow door, but large enough for the man who stood there—a little man with a colorless face and a quiet, abstracted look. His eyes were cold and keen, his features small, delicate, and regular. He had an erect back, and was dressed in a long-tailed coat, looking not much of a laird, and less of a farmer. He stood framed in the gray stone wall, in which odd little windows, dotted here and there at all heights and distances, revealed a wonderful arrangement of floors and rooms inside.

"Good morning, Mr. Fordyce!" said the doctor. "This is a bad business, but it might have been worse! Not a soul injured but one!"

"Souls don't commonly get injured by accident!" returned the laird, with a cold smile that was far from discourteous. "Stick to the body, doctor! There you know something!"

"It's a truth, laird!" answered the doctor, but added to himself, "Well, it's awful to hear the truth from some mouths!"

The laird spoke no word of either objection or welcome. They carried the poor fellow into the house, following its mistress to a room where, with the help of Meg, her one domestic, she soon had a bed prepared for him. Then the doctor rode away at full speed to fetch the appliances necessary, leaving the laird standing by the bed, with a look of mild dissatisfaction but not a whisper of opposition.

It was the guest chamber to which George Crawford had been carried, a room far more comfortable than a stranger might have believed possible from the aspect of the house. Everything in the room was old-fashioned and, having been dismantled, was not in apple-pie order; but it was rapidly and silently restored to its humble ideal. When the doctor returned with his assistant, he seemed both surprised and pleased at the change.

"He must have someone to sit up with him, Miss Fordyce," he said, when all was done.

"I will myself," she answered. "But you must give me exact direction, for I have done no nursing."

"If you will walk a little way with me, I will tell you all you need to know. He will sleep now, I think, for a short time. It is not a very awkward fracture," he continued as they went. "It might have been much worse! We shall have him about in a few weeks, but he will want the greatest care while the bones are uniting."

The laird turned from the bed and went to his study where, lost and old and pale, he walked up and down in the midst of his ancient volumes. Whatever his eyes fell upon, he turned from, as if he had no longer any pleasure in it; presently he stole back to the room where the sufferer lay. On tiptoe, with a caution suggestive of being near a wild beast asleep, he crept to the bed, looked down on his unwelcome guest with an expression of sympathy crossed with dislike, and shook his head slowly and solemnly, like one injured but forgiving.

His eye fell upon the young man's wallet. It had fallen from his coat as they undressed him, and was on the table by his bedside. He caught it up just as Alexa reentered.

"How is he, father?" she asked.

"He is fast asleep," answered the laird. "How long does the doctor think he will have to be here?"

"I did not ask him," she replied.

"That was an oversight, my child," he returned. "It is of consequence we should know the moment for his removal."

"We shall know it in good time. The doctor called it an affair of weeks—or months—I forget. But you shall not be troubled, father. I will attend to him."

"But I *am* troubled, Alexa! You do not know how little money I have!"

Again he retired—slowly, shut his door, locked it, and began to search the wallet. He found certain bank notes, and made a discovery concerning its owner.

While Crawford lay in a half-slumber, with the help of Meg, Alexa continued making the chamber more comfortable. Chintz curtains now veiled the windows which, for all their narrowness, admitted too much light; and an old carpet deadened the sound of footsteps on the creaking boards, for the bones of a house do not grow silent with age. Now a fire burned in the antique grate and was a soul to the chamber which was chilly, looking to the north, and with walls so thick that it took half the summer to warm them through. Old Meg, moving to and fro, kept shaking her head like her master, as if she also were in the secret of some house-misery; but she was only indulging the funereal temperament of an ancient woman.

As Alexa had run through the heather that morning, she had looked not altogether unlike a peasant; her shoes were strong, her dress was short; but now she came and went in a soft-colored gown. She did not seem to belong to what is called society, but she looked dignified and at times almost stately, with an expression of superiority that was not strong enough to make her handsome face unpleasing.

The day crept on. The invalid was feverish, though his nurse obeyed the doctor minutely. She had her tea brought to her; but when the supper hour arrived, she went to join her father in the kitchen.

Chapter 5.

AFTER SUPPER

They always ate in the kitchen. Strange to say, there was no dining room in the house, though there was a sweetly old-fashioned drawing room. The servant was with the sufferer, but Alexa's thoughts were too much in the sick room to know that she was even eating her porridge and milk. The laird partook but sparingly, on the ground that the fare tended to fatness, which affliction of age he congratulated himself on having hitherto escaped. They ate in silence, but not a glance of her father that might indicate a want escaped the daughter. When the meal was ended, and the old man had given thanks, Alexa put on the table a big black Bible, which her father took with solemn face and reverent gesture. In the course of his nightly reading of the New Testament, he had come to the twelfth chapter of St. Luke, with the Lord's Parable of the Rich Man whose soul was required of him; he read it beautifully, with an expression that seemed to indicate a sense of the Lord meaning what He said.

"We will omit the psalm this evening for the sake of the sufferer," he said, having ended the chapter. "The Lord will have mercy and not sacrifice."

They rose from their chairs and knelt on the stone floor. The old man prayed with much tone and expression, and I think meant all he said, though none of it seemed to spring from fresh need or new thankfulness; for he used only the old stock phrases, which flowed freely from his lips. He dwelt much on the merits of the Saviour; he humbled himself as the chief of sinners, whom it must be a satisfaction to God to cut off, but a greater satisfaction to spare for the sake of One whom He loved. Plainly the man counted it a most important thing to stand well with Him who had created him. When they rose, Alexa looked formally solemn, but the wan face of her father shone; his psyche, if not his ego,[1] had prayed, and he felt comfortable. He sat down and looked fixedly, as if into eternity, but perhaps it was into vacancy; they are much the same to most people.

"Come into the study for a moment, Lexy, if you please," he said, rising at length. His politeness to his daughter, and indeed to all that came near him, was one of the most notable points in his behavior.

Alexa followed the slender black figure up the stair, which consisted of about a dozen steps, filling the entrance from wall to wall with a width of some twelve feet. Between it and the outer door there was but room for the door of the kitchen on the one hand, and that of a small closet on the other. At the top of the stair was a wide space, a sort of irregular hall, more like an out-of-doors court indoors, paved with large flat stones into which projected the other side of the rounded mass, bordered by the grassy enclosure.

The laird turned to the right, and passed through a door into a room which had but one small window that was hidden by bookcases. Naturally it smelled musty, of old books and decaying bindings, an odor not unpleasant to some nostrils. He closed the door behind him, placed a chair for his daughter, and set himself in another by a deal table upon which were books and papers.

"This is a sore trial, Alexa!" he said with a sigh.

"It is indeed, father—for the poor young man!" she returned.

"True, but it would be selfish indeed to regard the greatness of his suffering as rendering our trial the less. It is to us a more serious matter than you seem to think. It will cost much more than, in the present state of my finances, I can afford to pay. You little think . . ."

"But, father," interrupted Alexa, "how could we help it?"

"He might have been carried elsewhere!"

"With me standing there? Surely not, father! Even Andrew Ingram offered to receive him."

"Why did he not take him then?"

"The doctor wouldn't hear of it. And I wouldn't hear of it either."

"It was ill-considered, Lexy. But what's done is done—though, alas, not paid for!"

"We must take the luck as it comes, father."

"Alexa," rejoined the laird with solemnity, "you ought never to mention luck. There is no such thing. It was either for the young man's sins or to prevent worse, or for necessary discipline, that the train was overturned. The cause is known to *Him*. All are in His hands, and we must beware of attempting to take any out of His hands, for it cannot be done."

"Then, father, if there be no chance, our part was ordered too. So there is the young man in our spare room, and we must receive our share of the trouble as from the hand of the Lord."

"Certainly, my dear! It was the expense I was thinking of. I was only lamenting—bear me witness, I was not opposing—the will of the Lord. A man's natural feelings remain."

"If the thing is not to be helped, let us think no more about it!"

"It is the expense, my dear! Will you not let your mind rest for a moment upon the fact? I am doing my utmost to impress it upon you. For other expenses there is always something to show; for this there will be nothing, positively nothing!"

"Not the mended leg, father?"

"The money will vanish, I tell you, as a tale that is told."

"It is our life that vanishes that way!"

"The simile suits either. So long as we do not use the words of Scripture irreverently, there is no harm in making a different application of them. There is no irreverence here; next to the grace of God, money is the thing hardest to get and hardest to keep. If we are not wise with it, the grace—I mean the money—will not go far."

"Not so far as the next world, anyhow!" said Alexa as if to herself.

"How dare you, child! The Redeemer tells us to make friends of the mammon of unrighteousness, that when we die it may receive us into everlasting habitations."

"I read the passage this morning, father; it is *they*, not *it*, that will receive you. And I have heard that it ought to be translated, 'Make friends *with* or *by means of* the mammon of unrighteousness.' "

"I will reconsider the passage. We must not lightly change even the translated word!"

The laird had never thought that it might be of consequence to him one day to have friends in the other world. Neither had he reflected that the Lord did not regard the obligation of gratitude as ceasing with this life.

Alexa had reason to fear that her father made a friend *of*, and never a friend *with*, the mammon of unrighteousness. At the same time, the halfpenny he put in the plate every Sunday must go a long way if it was not estimated, like that of the poor widow, according to the amount he possessed, but according to the difficulty he found in parting with it.

"After weeks, perhaps months, of nursing and food and doctor's stuff," resumed the laird, "he will walk away, and we shall see not the smallest coin of the money he carries with him. The visible will become the invisible, the present the absent!"

"The little it will cost you, father—"

"Hold there, my child! If you call any cost little, I will not hear a word more; we should be but running a race from different points to different goals! It will cost—that is enough! How much it will cost *me*, you cannot calculate, for you do not know what money stands for in my eyes. There are things before which money is insignificant!"

"Those dreary old books!" said Alexa to herself, casting a glance on the shelves that filled the room from floor to ceiling, and from wall to wall.

"What I was going to say, father," she returned, "was that I have a little money of my own, and this affair shall cost you nothing. Leave me to contrive. Would you tell him his friends must pay his board, or take him away? It would be a nice anecdote in the annals of the Fordyces of Potlurg!"

"At the same time, what more natural?" rejoined her father. "His friends must in any case be applied to! I learn from his wallet—"

"Father!"

"Content yourself, Alexa. I have a right to know whom I receive under my roof. Besides, have I not learned thereby that the youth is a sort of connection?"

"You don't mean it, father?"

"I do mean it. His mother and yours were first cousins."

"That's not a connection—it's a close kinship!"

"Is it?" said the laird dryly.

"Anyhow," pursued Alexa, "I give you my word you shall hear nothing more of the expense."

She bade her father good-night, returned to the bedside of her patient, and released Meg from her duty.

Chapter 6.

THE LAIRD AND THE LADY

Thomas Fordyce was a tendril from the root of a very old family tree; born in poverty and with great pinching of his father and mother and brothers and sisters, he was educated for the church. But from pleasure in scholarship, from archaeological tastes, a passion for the arcana of history, and a strong love of literature, although not of the highest kind, he had settled down as a schoolmaster, and in his calling had excelled. By all who knew him he was regarded as an accomplished, amiable, and worthy man.

When his years were verging on the undefined close of middle age, he saw the lives between him and the family property, one by one, wither at the touch of death, until at last there was no one but himself and his daughter to succeed. He was at the time the head of a flourishing school in a large manufacturing town; and it was not without some regret, though with more pleasure, that he yielded his profession and retired to Potlurg.

Greatly dwindled as he found the property, and much and long as it had been mismanaged, it was yet of considerable value, and worth wise care. The result of the labor he spent upon it was such that it had now for years yielded him, if not a large rental, one far larger at least than his daughter imagined. But the sinking of the schoolmaster into a laird seemed to work ill for the man, and good only for the land. I say *seemed*, because what we call degeneracy is often but the unveiling of what was there all the time. The evil we are, we become.

If I have in me the tyrant or the miser, there he is, and such am I, as surely as if the tyrant or the miser were even now visible to the wondering dislike of my neighbors. I do not say the characteristic is at first so strong, or would be so hard to change as by its revealing development it must become; but it is there, alive, as an egg is alive; and by no means inoperative like a mere germ, but exercising real though hidden influence on the rest of my character. Therefore, except the growing vitality be in the process of killing these ova of death, it is for the good of the man that they should be so far developed as to show their existence. If the man does not then starve and slay them, they will drag him to the judgment seat of a fiery indignation.

For the laird, Nature could ill replace the human influences that had surrounded the schoolmaster; and the enlargement both of means and leisure enabled him to develop by indulgence a passion for a peculiar kind of possession, which, however refined in its objects, was yet but a branch of the worship of Mammon. It suits the enemy just as well, I presume, that a man should give his soul for rare coins as for money. In consequence he was growing more and more withdrawn, ever filling less the part of a man which is to be a hiding place from the wind, a covert from the tempest. He was living more and more for himself, and thereby losing his life. Dearly as he loved his daughter, he was, by slow fallings away, growing ever less of a companion, less of a comfort, less of a necessity to her, and requiring less and less of her for the good or ease of his existence. We wrong those near us in being independent of them. God Himself would not be happy without His Son. We ought to lean on each other, giving and receiving—not as weaklings, but as lovers. Love is strength as well as need. Alexa was more able to live alone than most women; therefore, it was the worse for her. Too satisfied with herself, too little uneasy when alone, she did not know that she was then not in good enough company. She had what most would call a strong nature, but she did not know what weaknesses belong to, and grow out of, such strength as hers.

The remoter scions of a family tree are often those who make most account of it; the schoolmaster's daughter knew more about the Fordyces of Potlurg, and cared more for their traditions, than any who in more recent years reaped its advantages or shared its honors. Interest in the channel down which one has slid into the world is reasonable, and may be elevating; with Alexa it passed beyond good and wrought for evil. Proud of a family with a history and occasionally noted in the annals of the country, she regarded herself as the superior of all whom she had hitherto met. To the poor, to whom she was invariably and essentially kind, she was less condescending than to such as came nearer her own imagined standing; she was constantly aware that she belonged to the elect of the land! Society took its revenge, for the rich tradespeople looked down upon her as the schoolmaster's daughter. Against their arrogance her indignation buttressed her lineal superiority with her mental superiority, until at last, the pride of family was a personal arrogance. And now at length, she was in her natural position as heiress of Potlurg!

She was religious, if one might be called religious who felt no immediate relation to the Source of her being. She felt bound to defend, so far as she honestly could, the doctrines concerning God and His ways transmitted by the elders of her people; to this much, and little more, her religion toward God amounted. But she had a strong sense of obligation to do what was right.

Her father gave her so little money to spend that she had to be very careful with her housekeeping, and they lived in the humblest way. For her person she troubled him as little as she could, believing him, from the half-statements and hints he gave, and his general carriage toward life, not a little oppressed by lack of money, nor suspecting his difficulties to be induced by himself. In this regard it had come to be understood between them that the produce of the poultry yard was Alexa's own; and to some little store of money she had thus gathered, she mainly trusted for the requirements of her invalid. To this her father could not object, though he did not like it; he felt what was hers to be his, more than he felt what was his to be hers.

Alexa had not learned to place value on money beyond its use; yet, she was not therefore free from the service to Mammon. She looked to it as to a power essential, not derived; she did not see it as God's creation, but merely as an existence, thus making a creation of God into the Mammon of unrighteousness. She did not, however, cling to it, but was ready to spend it. At the same time, had George Crawford been less handsome or less

30

of a gentleman, she would not have been so ready to devote to him the contents of her little secret drawer.

The discovery of her relationship to the young man waked a new feeling. She had never had a brother, had never known a cousin, and had avoided the approach of those young men who, of inferior position in her eyes, had sought to be friendly with her. Now here was one thrown helplessly on her care, with necessities enough to fill the gap between his real relation to her and that of the brother after whom she had sighed in vain! It was a new and delightful sensation to have a family claim on a young man—a claim, the material advantage of which was all on his side, the devotion all on hers. She was invaded by a flood of tenderness toward him. Was he not her cousin, a gentleman, and as helpless as any newborn child? Nothing should be wanting that a strong woman could do for a powerful man!

Chapter 7.

THE COUSINS

George Crawford was in excellent health when the accident occurred, and so when he began to recover, his restoration was rapid. The process, however, was still long enough to compel the cousins to know more of each other than many months of ordinary circumstance would have made possible.

George, feeling neither the need nor the joy of their kinship so much as Alexa, disappointed her by the coolness of his response to her communication of the fact; and as they were both formal—that is, less careful as to the reasonable than to the conventional—they were not very ready to fall in love. Such people may learn all about each other, and not come near enough for love to be possible between them. Some people draw near at once, and at once decline to love, remaining friends the rest of their lives. Others love at once; and some take a whole married life to come near enough, and at last love. But the reactions of need and ministration can hardly fail to breed tenderness, and disclose the best points of character.

The cousins were both handsome and—which was of more consequence—each thought the other handsome. They found their religious opinions closely coincident—nor any wonder, for they had gone for years to identical branches of the same church every Sunday, had been regularly pumped upon from the same reservoir, and had drunk the same arguments concerning things true and untrue.

George found that Alexa had plenty of brains, a cultivated judgment, some knowledge of literature, and that there was no branch of science with which she had not some little acquaintance or interest. Her father's teaching was beyond any he could have procured for her, and what he taught she had learned; for she had a love of knowing, a tendency to growth, a capacity for seizing real points, though as yet perceiving next to nothing of their relation to human life and hope. She believed herself a judge of verse; but in truth, her knowledge of poetry was limited to its outer forms, of which she had made good studies with her father. She had learned the *how* before the *what,* knew the body before the soul—could tell good binding but not bad leather—in a word, knew verse, but not poetry.

She understood nothing of music, but George did not miss that; he was more sorry she did not know French, not for the sake of its literature, but because of showing herself an educated woman.

Diligent in business, though not fervent in spirit, she was never idle. But there are other ways than idleness to waste time. Alexa was continually "improving herself," a big phrase for a small matter; she had not learned that to do the will of God is the *only* way to improve oneself. She would have scorned the narrowness of any who told her so, not understanding what the will of God means.

She found that her guest and cousin was a man of some position; George occupied a place of trust in the bank and, though not yet admitted to a full knowledge of its more important transactions, hoped soon to be made a partner. Alexa wondered that her father never should have mentioned the relationship. The fact was that, in a time of poverty, the schoolmaster had made to George's father the request of a small loan without security, and the banker had behaved as a rich relation and a banker was pretty sure to behave.

And so, when his father came to Potlurg to see George, the laird declined to appear, and the banker contented himself thereafter with Alexa's reports.

Chapter 8.

GEORGE AND THE LAIRD

Alexa's money was nearly exhausted, and most of her chickens had been devoured by the flourishing convalescent; but not yet would the doctor allow him to return to business.

One night the atmosphere was electric—heavy, sultry, and unrefreshing—and George could not sleep. There came a terrible burst of thunder, then a bannered spear of vividest lightning lapped the house in its flashing folds, and the simultaneous thunder was mingled with the sound, as it seemed, of the fall of some part of the building. George sat up in bed and listened. All was still. He must rise and see what had happened, and whether anyone was hurt! He might meet Alexa—a talk with her would be a pleasant episode in his sleepless night! He got into his dressing gown, and taking his stick, walked softly from the room.

His door opened immediately on the top of the stair. He stood and listened until another flash came and lighted up the space around him, with its walls of many angles. When the darkness was returned and the dazzling gone, and while the thunder yet bellowed, he caught the glimmer of a light under the door of the study, and made his way toward it over the worn slabs. He knocked, but there was no answer. He pushed the door, and saw that the light came from behind a projecting bookcase. He hesitated a moment, and glanced about him.

A little clinking sound came from somewhere. He stole nearer the source of the light—a thief might be there! He

34

peeped round the end of the bookcase and saw the laird kneeling before an open chest. He had just counted a few pieces of gold, and was putting them away. He turned over his shoulder a face deathly pale, and his eyes for a moment stared blank. Then with a shivering smile he rose. He had a worn dressing gown over his nightshirt, and looked a thread of a man.

"You take me for a miser?" he said, trembling, and stood expecting an answer.

Crawford was bewildered. What business had he there?

"I am *not* a miser!" resumed the laird. "A man may count his money without being a miser!" Still trembling, he stood and stared at his guest, either too much startled or too gentle to find fault with his intrusion.

"I beg your pardon, laird," said George. "I knocked, but receiving no answer, feared something was wrong."

"Why are you out of bed—and you an invalid?" returned Mr. Fordyce.

"I heard a heavy fall, and feared the lightning had done some damage."

"We shall see about that in the morning, and in the meantime had better go to bed," said the laird.

They turned together toward the door.

"What a multitude of books you have, Mr. Fordyce!" remarked George. "I had not a notion of such a library in the county!"

"I have been a lover of books all my life," returned the laird. "And they gather, they gather!" he added.

"Your love draws them," said George.

"The storm is over, I think," said the laird.

He did not tell his guest that there was scarcely a book on those shelves not sought after by book buyers; not one that was not worth money in the book market. Here and there the dulled gold of a fine antique binding returned the gleam of the candle, but any gathering of old law or worthless divinity would have looked much the same.

"I should like to glance over them," said George. "There must be some valuable volumes among so many!"

"Rubbish! Rubbish!" rejoined the old man testily, almost hustling him from the room. "I am ashamed to hear it called a library."

It seemed to Crawford, as again he lay awake in his bed, an altogether strange incident. A man may count his money when he pleases; but nonetheless must it seem odd that he should do so in the middle of the night, and with such a storm flashing and roaring about him, apparently unheeded. The next morning he got his cousin to talk about her father, but drew from her nothing to cast light on what he had seen.

Chapter 9.

IN THE GARDEN

Only a small portion remained of the garden, which had been the pride of many owners of the place. It was strangely antique, haunted with a beauty both old and wild, the sort of garden the children of heaven might play in when men sleep.

In a little arbor tent of honeysuckle in a cloak of sweet peas, constructed by an old man who had seen the garden grow less and less through successive generations, sat George and Alexa—two highly respectable young people, Scots of Scotland, like Jews of Judea, well satisfied in their own worthiness. How they found their talk interesting, I can scarce think. I should have expected them to be driven by very dullness to the pursuit of love; but the one was too prudent to initiate it, the other too staid to entice it. Yet, people on the borders of love being on the borders of poetry, they had fallen to talking about a certain new poem, concerning which George had an opinion to give, having read several notices of it.

"You should tell my father about it, George," said Alexa. "He is the best judge I know."

She did not realize that it was little more than the grammar of poetry the schoolmaster had ever given himself to understand. His best criticism was to show phrase calling to phrase across gulfs of speech.

The little iron gate, whose hinges were almost gone with rust, creaked and gnarred as it slowly opened to admit Andrew. He advanced with the long, slow, heavy step suggestive of nailed

37

shoes; but his hazel eyes had an outlook like that of an eagle from its eyrie, and seemed to dominate his being, originating rather than directing its motions. He had a russet-colored face, much freckled; hair so dark red as to be almost brown; a large, well-shaped nose, a strong chin; and a mouth of sweetness whose smile was peculiarly its own, having in it at once the mystery and the revelation of Andrew Ingram. He took off his cap as he drew near, and held it as low as his knee, while he stood waiting with something of the air of an old-fashioned courtier. His clothes—all but his coat, which was of some blue stuff and his Sunday one—were of a large-ribbed corduroy. For a moment no one spoke. He colored a little, but kept silent, his eye on the lady.

"Good morning, Andrew!" she said at length. "There was something, I forget what, you were to call about! Remind me, will you?"

"I did not come before, ma'am, because I knew you were occupied. And even now it does not greatly matter."

"Oh, I remember! The poem! I am very sorry, but I had so much to think of that it went quite out of my mind."

An expression half-amused, half-shy, without a trace of mortification, for an instant shadowed the young man's face.

"I wish you would let me have the lines again, ma'am! Indeed I should be obliged to you!" he said.

"Well, I confess they might first be improved! I read them one evening to my father, and he agreed with me that two or three of them were not quite rhythmical. But he said it was a fair attempt, and for a working man very creditable."

What Andrew was thinking it would have been hard to gather from his smile; but I believe it was that, if he had himself read the verses aloud, the laird would have found no fault with their rhythm. His attitude seemed more that of patient, respectful amusement than anything else.

Alexa rose, but then resumed her seat, saying, "As the poem is a religious one, there can be no harm in handing it to you on Sunday after church—that is," she added meaningly, "if you will be there!"

"Give it to Dawtie, if you please, ma'am," replied Andrew.

"Ah!" returned Miss Fordyce, in a tone almost of rebuke.

"I seldom go to church, ma'am," said Andrew, reddening a

little, but losing no sweetness from his smile.

"I understand as much. It is very wrong! *Why* don't you?"

Andrew was silent.

"I wish you to tell me," persisted Alexa, with a peremptoriness which came of the schoolmaster. She had known him too as her father's pupil.

"If you will have it, ma'am, I not only learn nothing from Mr. Smith, but I think much that he says is not true."

"Still, you ought to go for the sake of example."

"Do wrong to make other people follow my example? Can that be to do right?"

"*Wrong* to go to church! What *do* you mean? Wrong to pray with your fellowmen?"

"Perhaps the hour may come, ma'am, when I shall be able to pray with my fellowmen, even though the words they use seem addressed to a tyrant, not to the Father of Jesus Christ. But at present I cannot. I might endure to hear Mr. Smith say evil things *concerning* God, but the evil things he says *to* God make me quite unable to pray, and I feel like a hypocrite!"

"Whatever you may think of Mr. Smith's doctrines, it is presumptuous to set yourself up as too good to go to church."

"I must bear the reproach, ma'am. I cannot consent to be a hypocrite in order to avoid being called one!"

Either Miss Fordyce had no answer to this, or did not choose to give any. She was not troubled that Andrew would not go to church, but offended at the unhesitating decision with which he set her counsel aside. Andrew made her a respectful bow, turned away, put on his bonnet which he had held in his hand all the time, and passed through the garden gate.

"Who is the fellow?" asked George, partaking sympathetically of his companion's annoyance.

"He is Andrew Ingram, the son of a small farmer, one of my father's tenants. He and his brother work with their father on the farm. They are quite respectable people. Andrew is conceited, but has his good points. He imagines himself a poet, and indeed his work has merit. The worst of him is that he sets up for being better than other people."

"Not an unusual fault with the self-educated!"

"He does go on educating himself, I believe, but he had a good start to begin with. My father took many pains with him at

school. Andrew helped to carry you here after the accident—
and would have taken you to his father's if I would have let
him."

George cast on her a look of gratitude. "Thank you for
keeping me," he said. "But I wish I had taken some notice of his
kindness!"

Chapter 10

ANDREW INGRAM

Of the persons in my narrative, Andrew is the simplest, and, therefore, the hardest to be understood by an ordinary reader. I must take up his history from a certain point in his childhood.

One summer evening, he and his brother, Sandy, were playing together on a knoll in one of their father's fields. Andrew was ten years old, and Sandy a year younger. The two quarreled, and with the spirit of ancestral borderers waking in them, they fell to blows. The younger was the stronger for his years, and they were punching each other with relentless vigor, when suddenly they heard a voice, and stopped their fight. They saw before them a humble-looking peddler with a pack on his back. They stood abashed before him, dazed with the blows they had received, and not a little ashamed; for they were well brought up, their mother being an honest disciplinarian, and their father never interfering with what she judged right. The sun was near setting, and shone with level rays full on the peddler; but when they thought of him afterward, they seemed to remember more light on his face than that of the sun. Their conscience bore him witness, and his look awed them. Involuntarily they turned from him, seeking refuge with each other. "His eyes shone so!" they said, but immediately they turned to see him again.

Sandy knew the pictures in *Pilgrim's Progress,* and Andrew had read it through more than once; when they saw that the man had an open book in his hand, and when they heard him begin to read from it, standing there in the sun, they thought it must be Christian waiting for Evangelist. It is impossible to say how much is fact and how much is imagination in what children recollect, for the one must almost always supplement the other; but they were quite sure that the words he read were these, "And lo, I am with you always, even to the end of the world!" The next thing they remembered was walking slowly down the hill in the red light, and all at once waking up to the fact that the man was gone, they did not know when or where. But their arms were round each other's necks, and they were full of a strange awe. Then Andrew saw something on Sandy's face.

"Eh, Sandy!" he cried. "It's blood!" and burst into tears.

It was his own blood, not Sandy's—which discovery relieved Andrew, and did not so greatly discompose Sandy.

They began at length to speculate on what had happened. One thing was clear—it was because they were fighting that the man had come; but it was not so clear who the man was. He could not be Christian, because Christian went over the river! Andrew suggested it might have been Evangelist, for he seemed always to be about. Sandy added his contribution to the idea, that he might have picked up Christian's bundle and been carrying it home to his wife. They came, however, to the conclusion that the stranger was the Lord Himself, and that the pack on His back was their sins, which He was carrying away to throw out of the world.

"Eh, wasna it fearful He should come by just when we was fighting!" said Sandy.

"Eh, na! It was a fine thing that! We might have been at it yet! But we willna now—will we ever, Sandy?"

"Na, that we willna!"

"For," continued Andrew, "He said, 'Lo, I am with you always!' And suppose He werena, we darena be that behind His back we wouldna be before His face!"

"Do you really think it *was* Him, Andrew?"

"Well," replied Andrew, "if the devil be going about like a roaring lion, seeking whom he may devour, as father says, it's no likely *He* would not be going about as well, seeking to hold him off of us!"

"Aye!" said Sandy.

"And now," asked the elder, "what are we to do?"

For Andrew, whom both father and mother judged the dreamiest of mortals, was in reality the most practical being in the whole parish—so practical that by and by people mocked him for a poet and a heretic, because he did the things which they said they believed. Most unpractical must every man appear who genuinely believes in the things that are unseen. The man called practical by the men of this world is he who busies himself building his house on the sand, while he does not even speak of a lodging in the inevitable beyond.

"What are we to do?" said Andrew. "If the Lord is going about like that, looking after us, we've surely got something to do looking after *Him!*"

There was no help in Sandy; and, with the reticence of children, it was well that neither thought of laying the case before their parents; the traditions of the elders would have ill agreed with the doctrine they were now under! Suddenly it came to Andrew's mind that the book they read at worship, and to which he had never listened, told all about Jesus.

He began that same book at the beginning, and grew so interested in the stories, that he forgot why he had begun to read it. One day, however, as he was telling Sandy about Jacob, Sandy said, "What a shame!" and Andrew's mind suddenly opened to the fact that he had got nothing yet out of the book. He threw it from him, echoing Sandy's words, "What a shame!" not of Jacob's behavior, but of the Bible's, which had all this time told them nothing about the Man that was going up and down the world, gathering up their sins and carrying them away in His pack! But then it dawned upon him that it was the New Testament that told about Jesus Christ, and they turned to that. It was well they asked no advice, for they would probably have been directed to the Epistle to the Romans, with explanations yet more foreign to the heart of Paul than false to his Greek. They began to read the story of Jesus as told by His friend Matthew, and when they had ended it, went on to the Gospel according to Mark.

But they had not read far when Sandy cried out, "Eh, Andrew, it's all the same thing over again!"

"Not altogether," answered Andrew. "We'll go on and see!"

Andrew came to the conclusion that it was so far the same

that he would rather go back and read the other again, for the sake of some particular things he wanted to make sure about. So the second time they read St. Matthew, and came to these words, "If two of you shall agree on earth as touching anything that they shall ask, it shall be done for them of My Father which is in heaven."

"There's two of us here!" cried Andrew, laying down the book. "Let's try it!"

"Try what?" said Sandy.

His brother read the passage again.

"Let the two of us ask Him for something!" concluded Andrew. "What will it be?"

"I wonder if it means only once, or maybe three times, like the three wishes!" suggested Sandy, who, like most Christians, would rather have a talk about it than do what he was told.

"We *might* ask for what would not be good for us!" returned Andrew.

"And make fools of ourselves!" assented Sandy, with the three wishes in his mind.

"Do you think He would give it to us then?"

"I don't know."

"But," pursued Andrew, "if we were so foolish as that old man and woman, it would be better to find it out and begin to grow wise! I'll tell you what we'll do; we'll make it our first wish, to know what's best to ask for, and then we can go on asking!"

"Yes, yes! Let us!"

"I fancy we'll have as many wishes as we like! Down on yer knees, Sandy!"

They kneeled together.

I fear there are not a few to say, "How ill-instructed the poor children were! Actually mingling the Gospel and the fairy tales!"

"Happy children," say I, "who could blunder into the very heart of the will of God concerning them, and *do* the thing at once that the Lord taught them, using common sense which God had given them and the fairy tale had nourished! The Lord of the promise is the Lord of all true parables and all good fairy tales."

Andrew prayed, "O Lord, tell Sandy and me what to ask for. We're unanimous."

They got up from their knees. They had said what they had to say, so why say more?

They felt rather dull. Nothing came to them. The prayer was prayed, and they could not make the answer. There was no use in reading more. They put the Bible away in a rough box where they kept it among rose leaves—ignorant priests of the lovely mystery of Him who was with them always—and without a word went each his own way, not happy, for were they not leaving Him under the elder tree, lonely and shadowy, where it was their custom to meet? Alas for those who must go to church to find Him, or who cannot pray unless in their closet!

They wandered about disconsolate, at school and at home, the rest of the day—at least Andrew did; Sandy had Andrew to lean upon! Andrew had Him who was with them always, but He seemed at the other end of the world. They had prayed, and there was no more of it!

In the evening, while it was yet light, Andrew went alone to the elder tree, took the Bible from its humble shrine, and began turning over its leaves.

"And why call ye Me, 'Lord, Lord,' and do not the things which I say?"

He read, and sank deep in thought. This is the way his thoughts went, "What things? What had He been saying? Let me look and see what He said, that I may begin to do it!"

He read all the chapter, and found it full of *tellings*. When he had read it before, he had not thought of doing one of the things Jesus said, for as plainly as He told him, he had not once thought he had any concern in the matter!

"I see!" he said. "We must begin at once to do what He tells us!"

He ran to find his brother.

"I've got it!" he cried. "I've got it!"

"What?"

"What we've got to do."

"And what is it?"

"Just what He tells us."

"We were doing that," said Sandy, "when we prayed Him to tell us what to pray for!"

"So we were! That's grand!"

"Then haven't we got to pray for anything more?"

"We'll soon find out—but first we must look for something to do!"

They began at once to search for things the Lord told them to do. And of all they found, the plainest and easiest was, "Whosoever shall smite thee on thy right cheek, turn to him the other also." This needed no explanation! It was as clear as the day to both of them!

The very next morning the schoolmaster who, though of a gentle disposition, was irritable, took Andrew for the offender in a certain breach of discipline, and gave him a smart box on the ear. Andrew, as readily as if it had been instinctively, turned to him the other cheek.

An angry man is an evil interpreter of holy things, and Mr. Fordyce took the action for one of rudest mockery, nor thought of the higher Master therein mocked—if it were mockery—as he struck the offender a yet smarter blow. Andrew stood for a minute like one dazed, but the red on his face was not that of anger; he was perplexed as to whether he ought now to turn the former cheek again to the striker. Uncertain, he turned away and went to his work.

Some will stop here to say, "But do you really mean to tell us we ought to take the words literally as Andrew did?" I answer, "When you have earned the right to understand, you will not need to ask me. To explain what the Lord means to one who is not obedient is the work of no man who knows His work."

It is but fair to say for the schoolmaster that when he found he had been mistaken, he tried to make up to the boy for it—not by confessing himself wrong, for who could expect that of only a schoolmaster—but by being kinder to him than before. Through this he came to like Andrew, and would teach him things out of the usual way, such as how to make different kinds of verse.

By and by Andrew and Sandy had a quarrel. Suddenly Andrew came to himself and cried, "Sandy! Sandy! He says we're to agree!"

"Does He?"

"He says we're to love one another, and we canna do that if we dinna agree!"

There came a pause.

"Perhaps after all you were in the right, Sandy!" said Andrew.

"I was just going to say that, when I think about it, perhaps I wasn't so much in the right as I thought I was!"

"It can't matter much which was in the right, when we were both in the wrong!" said Andrew. "Let's ask Him to keep us from caring which is in the right, and make us both try to be in the right. We don't often differ about what we are to ask for, Sandy!"

"No, we don't."

"It's me to take care of you, Sandy!"

"And me to take care of you, Andrew!"

Here was the nucleus of a church! Two stones laid on the foundation stone.

"Look here, Sandy!" said Andrew. "We must have another, and soon there'll be four of us!"

"How's that?" asked Sandy.

"I wonder that we never noticed it before! Here's what He says, 'For where two or three are gathered together in My name, there am I in the midst of them.' In that way, wherever He might be walking about, we could always find Him! He likes two, and His Father will hear the agreed prayer, but He likes three better, and that stands to reason, for three must be better than two! First one must love Him; and soon two can love Him better, because each one is helped by the other, and loves Him the more that he loves the other one! And soon comes the third, and there's more and more throwing of lights, and there's the Lord Himself in the midst of them! And three makes a better midst than two!"

Sandy could not quite follow the reasoning, but he had his own way of understanding.

"It's just like the story of Shadrach, Meshach, and Abednego!"[2] he said. "There was three of them, and so He made four! Eh, just think of Him being with us His very self!"

Now here was a church indeed! The idea of a third was the very principle of growth. They would meet together and say, "O Father of Jesus Christ, help us to be good like Jesus," and then Jesus Himself would make them one, and worship the Father with them! The next thing, as a matter of course, was to look about for a third.

"Dawtie!" cried both at once.

Dawtie was the child of a cottar-pair,[3] who had an acre or two

47

of their father's farm, and helped him with it. Her real name has not reached me; Dawtie means Darling, and is a common term of endearment. Dawtie was a dark-haired, laughing little darling with shy, merry manners and the whitest teeth, full of fun, but solemn in an instant. Her small feet were bare and black—except on Saturday nights and Sunday mornings—but full of expression, and perhaps really cleaner, from their familiarity with the sweet, all-cleansing air than such as hide the day long in socks and shoes.

Dawtie's specialty was love of the creatures. She had an undoubting conviction that every one of them with which she came into contact understood and loved her. She was the champion of the oppressed, without knowing it. Every individual necessity stood on its own merits and came to her fresh and sole, as if she had forgotten all that went before it. Like some boys, she had her pockets as well as her hands at the service of live things. But unlike any boy, she had in her love no admixture of natural history; it was not interest in animals with her, but a personal love to the individual animal, whatever it might be, that presented itself to the love-power in her.

It may seem strange that there should be three such children together. But their fathers and mothers for generations had been poor—which was a great advantage, as may be seen in the world by him who has eyes to see, and heard in the Parable of the Rich Man by him who has ears to hear. Also they were God-fearing, which was a far greater advantage, and made them honorable; for they would have scorned things that most Christians will do. Dawtie's father had a rare and keen instinct for detecting and avoiding that which is mean—not in others but in himself. To the shades and nuances of his own selfishness, which men of high repute and comfortable conscience would neither be surprised to find in their neighbors nor annoyed to find in themselves, he would give no quarter. Along with Andrew's father, he had, in childhood and youth, been under the influence of a simplehearted pastor, whom the wise and prudent laughed at as one who could not take care of himself, incapable as they were of seeing that like his Master, he laid down his life that he might take it again. He left God to look after him, that he might be free to look after God.

Little Dawtie had learned her catechism but, thank God, had

never thought about it or attempted to understand it—and so was prepared for becoming able in a few years more to understand the New Testament with the heart of a babe.

The brothers had not long to search before they came upon her, where she sat on the ground at the door of the turf cottage, feeding a chicken with oatmeal paste.

"What are you doing, Dawtie?" they asked.

"I'm tryin'," she answered, without looking up, "to hold the life in the chickie."

"What's the matter with it?"

"Nothing but the want of a mother."

"Is the mother of it dead?"

"Na, she's alive enough, but she has overmany bairns to help them all. Her wings willna cover them, and she drives this one away, and willna let it come near her."

"Such a cruel mother!"

"Na, she's no cruel. She only wants to make it come to me! She knew I would take it. Na, na, Flappy's a good mother! I know her well—she's one of our own! She knows me, or she would have kept the poor thing and done her best with her."

"I know Somebody," said Andrew, "that would spread out wings like a great hen over all the bairns, you and me and all, Dawtie!"

"That's my mother!" cried Dawtie, looking up and showing her white teeth.

"Na, it's a Man," said Sandy.

"It's my father, then!"

"Na, it's no. Would ye like to see Him?"

"Na, I'm no caring."

"Sandy and me's going to see Him someday."

"I'll go with ye, but I must take my chickie!"

She looked down where she had set the little bird on the ground; it had hobbled away and she could not see it!

"Eh," she cried, starting up, "ye made me forget my chickie with your questions! Its mother'll peck it!"

She darted off, and forsook the tale of the Son of man to look after His chicken. But presently she returned with it in her hands.

"Tell away," she said, resuming her seat. "What do they call Him?"

"They call Him the Father of Jesus Christ."

"I'll go with ye," she answered.

So the church was increased by a whole half—and the fraction of a chicken—a type of the groaning creation waiting for the sonship.

The three gathered to read and pray. And almost always there was some creature with them in the arms or hands of Dawtie. And if the Lord was not there too, then are we Christians most miserable, for we see a glory beyond all that man could dream, and it is but a dream! Whose dream?

They went on at other times with the usual employments and games of children. But there was this difference between them and most grown Christians, that when anything roused thought or question, they at once referred it to the words of Jesus, and having discovered His will, made haste to obey it. Because He gives the Spirit to them that obey Him, it naturally followed that they grew rapidly in the modes of their Master, learning to look at things as He looked at them, to think of them as He thought of them, to value what He valued, and despise what He despised—all in the simplest order of divine development, in utter accord with highest reason and turning on their continuous effort to obey.

They did not have any regular time of meeting. Andrew always took initiative in assembling the church, and when he called they came together. Then he would read from the story, and communicate any discovery he had made concerning what Jesus would have them do. Next, they would consult and settle what they should ask for; and then one of them, generally Andrew but sometimes Sandy, would pray. They made no formal utterance, but simply asked for what they needed. Here are some specimens of their petitions.

"O Lord, Sandy canna for the life of him understand the Rule of Three; please, Lord, help him."

"O Lord, I dinna know anything I want the day. Please give us what we need, and what Ye want us to have, without our asking it."

"Lord, help us; we're bad-tempered the day, and Ye wouldna have us that."

"Lord, Dawtie's mother's head is sore; make her better, if Ye please."

When their prayers were ended, Andrew would say, "Sandy, have you found anything He says?" And thereupon, if he had, Sandy would speak. Dawtie never said a word, but sat and listened with her big eyes, generally stroking some creature in her lap. Surely the part of every superior is to help the life in the lower!

Once the question arose in their assembly of three—plus a bird whose leg Dawtie had put in splints—what became of the creatures when they died. They concluded that the sparrow God cared for must be worth caring for, and they could not believe He had made it to last only such a little while as its life in this world. Thereupon they agreed to ask the Lord that when they died, they might have again a certain dog, an ugly little white mongrel of which they had been very fond. All their days thereafter they were more or less consciously looking forward to the fulfillment of this petition. Their hope strengthened with the growth of their ideal; and when they had to give up any belief, it was to take a better in its place.

They yielded at length the notion that the peddler was Jesus Christ; but they never ceased to believe that he was God's messenger, or that the Lord was with them always. They would not insist that He was walking about on the earth; but to the end of their days they cherished the hope that they might, even without knowing it, look upon the face of the Lord in that of some stranger passing in the street, mingling in a crowd, or seated in a church. For they knew that all the shapes of man belong to Him and that, after He rose from the dead, there were several occasions on which He did not at first look like Himself to those to whom He appeared.

The childlike, the essential, the divine notion of serving with their everyday will and being the will of the Living One, who lived for them that they might live, as once He had died for them that they might not die, ripened in them to a Christianity that saw God everywhere, saw that everything ought to be done as God would have it done, and that nothing but injustice had to be forsaken to please Him. They were under no influence of what has been so well called *otherworldliness;* for they saw this world as much God's as that other world, saw that its work has to be done divinely, that this world is the beginning of the world to come. It was to them all one world, with God in it, all in all; therefore the best work for the other world was the work of this world.

Such was the boyhood of that Andrew Ingram whom Miss Fordyce now reproved for not setting the good example of going to church.

The common sense of the children rapidly developed after that, for there is no teacher like obedience, and no obstruction like its postponement. In after years, when their mothers came at length to understand that obedience had been so long the foundation of their lives, it explained to them many things that had seemed strange, and brought them to reproach themselves that they should have seemed strange.

It ought not to be overlooked that the whole thing was wrought in the children without directive influence of kindred or any neighbor. They imitated none. The galvanism of imitation is not the life of the spirit; where there is not love, the use of form is killing. And if anyone is desirous of spreading the truth, let him apply himself, like these children, to the doing of it. Not obeying the truth, he is doubly a liar pretending to teach it; if he obeys it already, let him obey it more. It is life that awakes life. All form of persuasion is empty except in vital association with regnant obedience. Talking and not doing is dry rot.

Cottage children are sometimes more fastidious about their food than children who have a greater variety; they have a more delicate perception and discrimination in the simple dishes on which they thrive. Andrew had a great dislike to lumps in his porridge; and when one day their mother had been less careful than usual in cooking it, he made a wry face at the first spoonful.

"Andrew," said Sandy, "take no thought for what ye eat."

It was a wrong interpretation, but a righteous use of the Word. Happy the soul that mistakes the letter only to get at the spirit!

Andrew's face smoothed itself, began to clear up, and broke at last into a sunny smile. He said nothing, but ate his full share of the porridge without a frown. This was practical religion; and if anyone judge it not worth telling, I count his philosophy worthless beside it. Such a doer knows more than such a reader will ever know, except that he take precisely the same way to learn. The children of God do what He would have them do, and are taught of Him.

A report at length reached the pastor, now an old man of ripe heart and true insight, that certain children in his parish "played at the Lord's Supper." He was shocked, and went to their parents. They knew nothing of the matter. The three children were sought, and the pastor had a private interview with them. From it he reappeared with a solemn, pale face, and a silent tongue. They asked him the result of his inquiry. He answered that he was not prepared to interfere; as he was talking with the children, the warning had come to him that there were necks and millstones. The next Sunday he preached a sermon from the text, "Out of the mouth of babes and sucklings, Thou hast perfected praise."

The fathers and mothers made inquisition of their children and found no desire to conceal. Wisely or not, they forbade the observance. It cost Andrew much thought whether he was justified in obeying them; but he saw that right and wrong in itself was not concerned, and that the Lord would have them obey their parents.

The bond between the children, altering in form as they grew, was never severed; nor was the lower creation ever cut off from its share in the petitions of any one of them. When they ceased to assemble as a community, they continued to act on the same live principles.

Gladly as their parents would have sent them to college, Andrew and Sandy had to leave school to work on the farm. But they carried their studies on from the point they had reached. When they could not get further without help, they sought and found it. For a year or two they went in the winter to an evening school; but it took so much time to go and come that they found they could make more progress by working at home. What help they sought went a long way, and what they learned they retained.

When the day's work was over, and also the evening meal, they went to the room their own hands had made convenient for study as well as for sleep, and there resumed the labor they had dropped the night before. Together they read Greek and mathematics, but Andrew worked mainly in literature, Sandy in mechanics. On Saturdays, Sandy generally wrought at some model, while Andrew read to him. On Sundays, they always read the Bible together for an hour or two.

The two brothers were not a little amused with Miss Fordyce's patronage of Andrew; but they had now been too long endeavoring to bring into subjection the sense of personal importance, to take offense at it.

Dawtie had gone into service as a housemaid, and they seldom saw her except when she came home for a day at the term. She was a grown woman now, but the same loving child as before. She counted the brothers her superiors, just as they counted the laird and his daughter their superiors. But whereas Alexa claimed the homage, Dawtie yielded where there was no thought of claiming it. The brothers regarded her as a sister. That she was poorer than they only made them the more watchful over her, and if possible the more respectful to her. So she had a rich return for her care of the chickens and kittens and puppies.

It has been necessary to tell so much of the previous history of Andrew, lest what remains to be told should perhaps be unintelligible or seem incredible without it. A character like his cannot be formed in a day; it must early begin to grow.

Chapter 11.

GEORGE AND ANDREW

George went home the day following the encounter in the garden. The next week he sent Andrew a note, explaining that when he saw him he did not know his obligation to him, and expressing the hope that when Andrew came to town, he would call upon him. This was hardly well, being condescension to one who was George's moral superior. Perhaps the worst evil in the sense of social superiority is the vile fancy that it alters human relation. George did not feel bound to make the same acknowledgment of obligation to one in humble position as to one in the same golden rank with himself! It says ill for social distinction if, for its preservation, such an immoral difference be essential. But Andrew was not one to dwell upon his rights. He thought it friendly of Mr. Crawford to ask him to call; therefore, although he had little desire to make his acquaintance, and grudged the loss of time—to no man so precious as to him who has a pursuit in addition to a calling—Andrew, being far stronger in courtesy than the man who invited him, took the first Saturday afternoon to go and see him.

Mr. Crawford the elder lived in some style, and his door was opened by a servant whose blatant adornment filled Andrew with a friendly pity; he judged that no man would submit to be dressed like that except from necessity. Yet the reflection sprang from no foolish and degrading contempt for household service. It is true Andrew thought no labor so manly as that in the earth, out of which grows everything that makes the loveliness or use of Nature; for by it he came in contact with the primaries of human life, and was God's fellow laborer, a helper in the world of the universe, knowing the ways of it and living in them. But nonetheless would he have done any service, and that cheerfully, which his own need or that of others might have required of him. The colors of a parrot, however, were not fit for a son of man, and hence Andrew's look of sympathy. His regard was met only by a glance of plain contempt, as the lackey, moved by the same spirit as his master, left him standing in the hall, to return presently and show him into the library, a room of mahogany, red morocco, and yellow calf, where George sat. He rose and shook hands with Andrew.

"I am glad to see you, Mr. Ingram," he said. "When I wrote I had but just learned how much I was indebted to you."

"I understand what you must mean," returned Andrew, "but it was scarce worth alluding to. Miss Fordyce had the better claim to serve you!"

"You call it nothing to carry a man of my size over a mile of heather?"

"I had help," answered Andrew, "and but for the broken leg," he added with a laugh, "I could have carried you well enough alone."

There came a pause, for George did not know what next to do with the farmer. So the latter spoke again, being unembarrassed.

"You have a grand library, Mr. Crawford! It must be fine to sit among so many books! It's just like a wine merchant's cellars—only here you can open and drink, and leave the bottles as full as before!"

"A good simile, Mr. Ingram!" replied George. "You must come and dine with me, and we'll open another sort of bottle!"

"You must excuse me there, sir! I have no time for that sort of bottle."

"I understand you read a great deal?"

"Weather permitting," returned Andrew.

"I should have thought if anything was independent of the weather, it must be reading!"

"Not a farmer's reading, sir. To him the weather is the word of God telling him whether to work or to read."

George was silent. To him the Word of God was the Bible!

"But you must read a great deal yourself, sir!" resumed Andrew, casting a glance round the room.

"The books are my father's!" said George.

He did not mention that his own reading came all in the library cart, except when he wanted some special information, for George was "a practical man." He read his Bible to prepare for his class in the Sunday School, and his Shakespeare when he was going to see a play. He would make the best of both worlds by paying due attention to both! He was religious but liberal.

His father was both a banker and an elder in the kirk, well reputed in and beyond his circle. He gave to many charities, largely to educational schemes. His religion was to hold by the traditions of the elders, and keep himself respectable in the eyes of money dealers. He went to church regularly, and always asked God's blessing on his food, as if it were a kind of general sauce. He never prayed God to make him love his neighbor, or help him to be an honest man. He "had worship" every morning, no doubt; but only a nonentity like his God could care for such prayers as his. George rejected his father's theology as false in logic and cruel in character; George knew just enough of God to be guilty of neglecting Him.

"When I am out all day, I can do with less reading, for then I have the 'book of knowledge fair,'" said Andrew, quoting Milton. "It does not take *all* one's attention to drive a straight furrow, or keep the harrow on the edge of the last bout!"

"You don't mean you can read your Bible as you hold the plow!" said George.

"No, sir," answered Andrew, amused. "A body could not well manage a book between the stilts of the plow. The Bible will keep till you get home; a little of it goes a long way. But Paul counted the book of creation enough to make the heathen to blame for not minding it. Never a wind wakes of a sudden, but it talks to me about God. And is not the sunlight the same that came out of the body of Jesus at His transfiguration?"

"You seem to have some rather peculiar ideas of your own, Mr. Ingram!"

"Perhaps, sir. For a man to have no ideas of his own is much the same as to have no ideas at all. A man cannot have the ideas of another man, any more than he can have another man's soul or another man's body!"

"That is dangerous doctrine."

"Perhaps we are not talking about the same thing! By *ideas*, I mean what a man orders his life by."

"Your ideas may be wrong!"

"The All-wise is my Judge."

"So much the worse, if you are in the wrong!"

"It is the only good, whether I be in the right or the wrong. Would I have my mistakes overlooked? What judge would I desire but the Judge of all the earth! Shall He not do right? And will He not set me right?"

"That is a most dangerous confidence!"

"It would be if there were any other judge. But it will be neither the church nor the world that will sit on the Great White Throne. He who sits there will not ask, 'Did you go to church?' or, 'Did you believe in this or that?' but, 'Did you do what I told you to?'"

"And what will you say to that, Mr. Ingram?"

"I will say, 'Lord, Thou knowest!'"

The answer checked George a little. "Suppose He should say you did not. What would you answer?"

"I would say, 'Lord, send me where I may learn.'"

"And if He should say, 'That is what I sent you into the world for, and you have not done it!' what would you say then?"

"I should hold my peace."

"You do what He tells you then?"

"I try."

"Does He not say, 'Forsake not the assembling of yourselves together'?"

"No, sir."

"No!"

"Somebody says something like it in the Epistle to the Hebrews."

"And isn't that the same?"

"The man who wrote it would be indignant at your saying so! Tell me, Mr. Crawford, what makes a gathering a church?"

"It would take me some time to arrange my ideas before I could answer you."

"Is it not the presence of Christ that makes an assembly a church?"

"Well?"

"Does He not say that where two or three are met in His name, there He is in the midst of them?"

"Yes."

"Then thus far will I justify myself to you, that, if I do not go to what you call *church*, I yet often make one of a company met in His name."

"He does not limit the company to two or three."

"Assuredly not. But if I find I get more help and strength with a certain few, why should I go with a multitude to get less? Will you draw a line other than the Master's? Why should it be more sacred to worship with five hundred or five thousand than with three? If He is in the midst of them, they cannot be wrongly gathered!"

"It *looks* as though you thought yourselves better than everybody else!"

"If it were so, then certainly He would not be one of the gathering!"

"How are you to know that He is in the midst of you?"

"If we are not keeping His commandments, He is not. But His presence cannot be *proved;* it can only be known. If He meets us, it is not necessary to the joy of His presence that we should be able to prove that He does meet us! If a man has the company of the Lord, he will care little whether another does or does not believe that he has."

"Your way is against the peace of the church! It fosters division."

"Did the Lord come to send peace on the earth? My way, as you call it, would make division, but division between those who *call* themselves His, and those who *are* His. It would bring together those that love Him. Company would merge with company that they might look on the Lord together. I don't believe Jesus cares much for what is called the 'visible church,' but He cares with His very Godhead for those who do as He tells them. They are His Father's friends; they are His elect by whom He will save the world. It is by those who obey, and by their obedience, that He will save those who do not obey, that is, will bring them to obey. It is one by one the world will pass to His side. There is no saving in the lump. If a thousand be converted at once, it is still every single lonely man that is converted."

"You would make a slow process of it!"

"If slow, yet faster than any other. All God's processes are slow. How many years has the world existed, do you imagine, sir?"

"I don't know. Geologists say hundreds and hundreds of thousands."

"And how many is it since Christ came?"

"Toward two thousand."

"Then we are but in the morning of Christianity! There is plenty of time. The day is before us."

"Dangerous doctrine for the sinner."

"Why? Time is plentiful for his misery, if he will not repent; plentiful for the mercy of God that would lead him to repentance. There is plenty of time for labor and hope, but none for indifference and delay. God *will* have His creatures good. They cannot escape Him."

"Then a man may put off repentance as long as he pleases."

"Certainly he may—at least as long as he can—but it is a fearful thing to try issues with God."

"I can hardly say I understand you."

"Mr. Crawford, you have questioned me in the way of kindly anxiety and reproof; that has given me the right to question you. Tell me, do you admit we are bound to do what our Lord requires?"

"Of course. How could any Christian man do otherwise?"

"Yet a man may say, 'Lord, Lord,' and be cast out! It is one thing to say we are bound to do what the Lord tells us, and another to do what He tells us! He says, 'Seek ye *first* the kingdom of God and His righteousness.' Mr. Crawford, are you seeking the kingdom of God *first,* or are you seeking money first?"

"We are sent into the world to make our living."

"Sent into the world, we have to seek our living; we are not sent into the world to seek our living, but to seek the kingdom and righteousness of God. And to seek a living is very different from seeking a fortune!"

"If you, Mr. Ingram, had a little wholesome ambition, you would be less given to judging your neighbors."

Andrew held his peace, and George concluded he had had the best of the argument, which was all he wanted; of the truth concerned he did not see enough to care about it. Andrew, perceiving no good was to be done, was willing to appear defeated; he did not value any victory of the truth, and George was not yet capable of being conquered by the truth.

"No!" resumed George. "We must avoid personalities. There are certain things all respectable people have agreed to regard as right; he is a presumptuous man who refuses to regard them. Reflect on it, Mr. Ingram."

The curious smile hovered about the lip of the plowman; when things to say did not come to him, he went nowhere to fetch them. Almost in childhood he had learned that when one is required to meet the lie, words are given him; when they are not, silence is better. A man who does not love the truth, but disputes for victory, is the swine before whom pearls must not be cast. Andrew's smile meant that it had been a waste of his time to call upon Mr. Crawford. But he did not blame himself, for he had come out of pure friendliness. He would have risen at once, but feared to seem offended. Crawford, therefore, with the rudeness of a superior, rose and asked, "Is there anything I can do for you, Mr. Ingram?"

"The only thing one man can do for another is to be at one with him," answered Andrew, rising.

"Ah, you are a socialist! That accounts for much!" said George.

"Tell me this," returned Andrew, looking him in the eyes. "Did Jesus ever ask of His Father anything His Father would not give Him?"

"Not that I remember," answered George, fearing a theological trap.

"He said once, 'I pray for them which shall believe in Me, that they all may be one, as Thou Father art in Me, and I in Thee, that they also may be one in Us!' No man can be one with another who is not one with Christ."

As Andrew left the house, a carriage drove up in which was Mr. Crawford the elder, home from a meeting of directors at which a dividend had been agreed upon—to be paid from the capital in preparation for another issue of shares.

Andrew walked home a little bewildered. "How is it," he said to himself, "that so many who would be terrified at the idea of not being Christians, and are horrified at any man who does not believe there is a God, are yet absolutely indifferent to what their Lord tells them to do if they would be His disciples? But may I not be in like case without knowing it? Do I meet God in my geometry? When I so much enjoy my Euclid, is it always God geometrizing to me? Do I feel as if I were talking with God every time I dwell upon any fact of His world of lines and circle and angles? Is it God with me, every time that the joy of life, of a wind or a sky or a lovely phrase, flashes through me? O my God," he broke out in speechless prayer as he walked. Those that passed said to themselves he was mad, for how, in such a world, could any but a madman wear a face of joy!

"O my God, Thou art all in all, and I have everything! The world is mine because it is Thine! I thank Thee, my God, that Thou hast lifted me up to see whence I came, to know to whom I belong, to know who is my Father and makes me His heir! I am Thine, infinitely more than mine own; and Thou art mine as Thou art Christ's!"

He knew his Father in the same way that Jesus Christ knows His Father. He was at home in the universe, neither lonely nor afraid.

Chapter 12.

THE CRAWFORDS

Through strong striving to secure his life, Mr. Crawford lost his, both in God's sense of loss and his own. For certain financial activities of his which now came to the public light, he narrowly escaped being put in prison, died instead, and was put into God's prison to pay the uttermost farthing. But he had been such a good Christian that his fellow Christians mourned over his failure and his death, not over his dishonesty! For did they not know that if by more dishonesty he could have managed to recover his footing, he would have repaid everything? One injunction only he obeyed—he provided for his own; of all the widows concerned in his bank, his widow alone was secured from want. And she, like a dutiful wife, took care that his righteous intention should be righteously carried out; not a penny would she give up to the paupers her husband had made.

The downfall of the house of cards took place a few months after George's return to its business. Not yet initiated to the mysteries of his father's transactions, still ignorant of what had long been threatening, he felt it as a terrible blow. But he was a man of action, and at once resolved to go to America, for at home he could not hold up his head!

He had often returned to Potlurg, and had been advancing in intimacy with Alexa; but now he would not show himself there unless he could appear as a man of decision—until he was on the point of departure. She would then be the more willing to believe his innocence of complicity in the deception that had led to his ruin! He would thus also manifest self-denial and avoid the charge of interested motives! He could not face the suspicion of being a suitor with nothing to offer! George had always taken the grand role—that of superior, benefactor, bestower—and he was powerful in condescension.

Not, therefore, until the night before he sailed did he go to Potlurg, where Alexa received him with a shade of displeasure.

"I am going away," he said abruptly, the moment they were seated.

Her heart gave a painful throb in her throat, but she did not lose her self-possession.

"Where are you going?" she asked.

"To New York," he replied. "I have a situation there—in an important house in Wall Street. *There* at least I am taken for an honest man! From your heaven I have fallen."

"No one falls from any heaven but has himself to blame!" rejoined Alexa.

"Where have I been to blame? I was not in my father's confidence. I knew nothing, positively nothing, of what was going on."

"Why then did you not come to see me?"

"A man who is neither beggar nor thief is not willing to look either."

"You would have come if you had trusted me!" she said.

"You must pardon pride in a ruined man!" he answered. "Now that I am starting tomorrow, I do not feel the same dread of being misunderstood."

"It was not kind of you, George! Knowing yourself fit to be trusted, why did you not think me capable of trusting?"

"But, Alexa! A man's own father!" For a moment he showed signs of an emotion he had seldom had to repress.

"I beg your pardon, George!" cried Alexa. "I am both stupid and selfish! Are you really going so far?" Her voice trembled.

"I am—but to return, I hope, in a very different position!"

"You would have me understand—?"

"That I shall then be able to hold up my head."

"Why should an innocent man ever do otherwise?"

"He cannot help seeing himself in other people's thoughts!"

"If we are in the right, ought we to mind what people think of us?" said Alexa.

"Perhaps not. But I will make them think of me as I choose!"

"How?"

"By compelling their respect."

"You mean to make a fortune?"

"Yes."

"Then it will be the fortune they respect! You will not be more worthy."

"I shall not."

"Is such respect worth having?"

"Not in itself."

"In what then? Why lay yourself out for it?"

"Believe me, Alexa, even the real respect of such people would be worthless to me. I only want to bring them to their marrowbones!"

The truth was that Alexa prized social position so dearly that she did not relish his regarding it as a thing at the command of money. Let George become as rich as an American, Alexa would never regard him as her equal! George worshiped money; Alexa worshiped birth and land.

Our own way of being wrought is all right in our own eyes; our neighbor's way of being wrought is offensive to all that is good in us. We are anxious therefore, kindly anxious, to pull the mote out of his eye, never thinking of the big beam in the way of the operation. Jesus labored to show us that our immediate business is to be right in ourselves. Until we are, even our righteous indignation is waste.

While he spoke, George's eyes were on the ground. His grand resolve did not give his innocence strength to look in the face of the woman he loved; he felt, without knowing why, that she was not satisfied with him. Of the paltriness of his ambition, he had no inward hint. The high resolves of a puny nature must be a laughter to the angels—the bad ones.

"If a man has no ambition," he resumed, feeling after her objection, "how is he to fulfill the end of his being? No sluggard ever made his mark! How would the world advance but for the men who have to make their fortunes? If a man finds his father has not made money for him, what is he to do but make it for himself? You would not have me all my life a clerk! If I had but known, I should by this time have been well ahead!"

Alexa had nothing to answer; it all sounded very reasonable!

65

Were not Scots everywhere taught it was the business of life to rise? In whatever position they were, was it not their part to get out of it? She did not see that it is in the kingdom of God only that we are bound to rise. We are born into the world not to rise in the kingdom of Satan, but out of it. And the only way to rise in the kingdom of God is to do the work given us to do. Whatever be intended for us, this is the only way to do it. We have not to promote ourselves, but to do our work. It is the Master of the feast who says, "Go up." If a man go up of himself, he will find he has mistaken the head of the table.

More talk followed, but neither cast any light, for neither saw the true question. George took his leave. Alexa said she would be glad to hear from him.

Alexa did not like the form of George's ambition—to gain money and so compel the respect of persons he did not himself respect. But was she clear of the money-disease herself? Would she have married a poor man, to go on as hitherto? Would she not have been ashamed to have George know how she had supplied his needs while he lay in the house—that it was with the poor gains of her poultry yard she fed him? Did it improve her moral position toward money that she regarded commerce with contempt—a remnant of the time when a noble treated merchants as a cottager did his bees?

Chapter 13.

DAWTIE

Is not the church supposed to be made up of God's elect? And yet
you find it hard to believe there should be three such persons
as Andrew and Sandy and Dawtie, so related, who agreed to ask
of God, and to ask neither riches nor love, but that God should
take His own way with them, that the Father should work His
will in them—that He would teach them what He wanted of
them and help them to do it? The church is God's elect, and yet
you cannot believe in three holy children? Do you protest, "Because they are represented as beginning to obey so young"?

"Then," I answer, "there can be no principle in the perfecting of praise out of the mouth of babes and sucklings, or in the
preference of them to the wise and prudent as the recipients of
divine revelation."

Dawtie never said much, but tried the more. With heartiness
she accepted what conclusions the brothers came to, so far as
she understood them; and what was practical she understood as
well as they, for she had in her heart the spirit of that Son of
man who chose a child to represent Him and His Father. Their
minds were so set on doing what they found in the Gospel, that
other words heard at church passed over them without even
rousing their intellect, and so vanished without doing any hurt.
Tuned to the truth by obedience, no falsehoods they heard
from pulpit partisans of God could make a chord vibrate in
response. Dawtie indeed heard nothing but the good that was
mingled with the falsehood and shone like a lantern through a

thick fog.

She was little more than a child when, to the dismay of her parents, she had to go out to service as a housemaid. Every half-year she came home for a day or so, and neither feared nor found any relation altered. At length, after several closely following changes in her employment, occasioned by no fault of hers, she was without a place. Miss Fordyce heard of it and proposed to Dawtie's parents that until she found another, she should help Meg who was growing old and rather blind; she would thus, she said, go on learning, and not be idling at home.

Dawtie's mother was not a little amused at the idea of anyone idling in her home, not to say Dawtie, whom idleness would have tried harder than any amount of work; but, if only that Miss Fordyce might see what sort of girl Dawtie was, she judged it right to accept her offer.

Dawtie had not been at Potlurg a week before Meg began to complain that she did not leave work enough to keep her warm. No doubt it gave her time for her book, but her eyes were not so good as they used to be, and she was apt to fall asleep over it and catch cold! But when her mistress proposed to send Dawtie away, Meg would not hear of it. So Alexa, who had begun to take an interest in Dawtie, set her to do things she had hitherto done herself, and began to teach her other things. Before three months were over, she was a necessity in the house, and to part with Dawtie seemed impossible. When a place about that time turned up, Alexa at once offered her wages, and so Dawtie became an integral portion of the laird's modest household.

The laird himself at length began to trust her as he had never trusted a servant, for he taught her to dust his precious books, which hitherto he had done himself, but of late had shrunk from, finding not a few of them worse than Pandora's box in liberating asthma at the merest unclosing.

Dawtie was now a grown woman, bright, gentle, playful, with loving eyes and a constant overflow of tenderness upon any creature that could receive it. She had small but decided and regular features whose prevailing expression was confidence— not in herself, for she was scarce conscious of herself even in the act of denying herself—but in the person upon whom her trusting eyes were turned. She was in the world to help—with no social sense beyond the idea that for help and nothing else did anyone exist. To be as the sun and the rain and the wind, as the flowers that lived for her and not for themselves, as the river that flowed and the heather that bloomed lovely on the bare moor in the autumn, such was her notion of being. That she had to take care of herself was a falsehood that never entered her brain. To do what she ought, and not do what she ought not, was enough on her part; God would do the rest!

I will not say she reasoned thus; to herself she was scarce a conscious object at all. Both bodily and spiritually she was in the finest health. If illness came, she would perhaps then discover a self with which she had to fight—I cannot tell; but my impression is that she had so long done the true thing, that illness would only develop unconscious victory, perfecting the devotion of her simple righteousness. It is because we are selfish, with that worst selfishness which is incapable of recognizing its own loathsomeness, that we have to be made ill. That they may leave the last remnants of their selfishness, are the saints themselves overtaken by age and death. Suffering does not cause the vile thing in us—that was there all the time; it comes to develop in us the knowledge of its presence, that it may be war with the knife between us and it. It was no wonder that Dawtie grew more and more a favorite at Potlurg.

She did not read much, but would learn by heart anything that pleased her, and then go saying or singing it to herself. She had the voice of a lark, and her song prevented many a search for her. Against that "rain of melody," not the pride of the laird nor the orderliness of the exschoolmaster ever put up an umbrella of rebuke. Her singing was so true, came so clear from the fountain of joy, and so plainly from no desire to be heard, that it gave no annoyance; while such was her sympathy that, although she had never yet suffered, you would, to hear her sing "My Nanie's Awa'!"[5] have thought her in truth mourning an absent lover, and familiar with every pang of heart-privation. Her cleanliness, clean even of its own show, was a heavenly purity; while so gently was all her spiriting done that the very idea of fuss died in the presence of her labor. To the self-centered, such a person soon becomes a nobody; the more dependent they are upon her unfailing ministration, the less they think of her. However, they have another way of regarding such in the high countries.

Alexa, who wondered at times that she could not interest her in the things she made her read, little knew how superior the girl's choice was to her own. Not knowing much of literature, what Dawtie liked was always of the best in its kind, and nothing without some best element could interest her at all. But she was not left either to her own sweet will or to the prejudices of her well-meaning mistress; however long the intervals that parted them, Andrew continued to influence her reading as from the first. A word now and a word then, with the books he lent or gave her, was sufficient. That Andrew liked this or that was enough to make Dawtie set herself to find in it what Andrew liked; and it was thus she became acquainted with most of what she learned by heart.

About two years before the time to which I have now brought my narrative, Sandy had given up farming to pursue the development of certain inventions of his which had met the approval of a man of means who, unable himself to devise, could yet understand a device; he saw that there was use and, consequently, money in them, and wisely put it in Sandy's power to perfect them. In consequence, he was but little at home; and when Dawtie went to see her parents, as she could much oftener now, Andrew and she generally met without a third. However many weeks might have passed, they always met as if they had only parted the night before. There was neither shyness nor forwardness in Dawtie. Perhaps a livelier rose might tinge her sweet round cheek when she saw Andrew; perhaps a brighter spark shone in the pupil of Andrew's eye; but they met as calmly as two prophets in the secret of the universe, neither anxious nor eager. The old relation between them was the more potent that it made so little outward show.

"Have you anything for me, An'rew?" Dawtie would say, in the strong dialect which her sweet voice made so pleasant to those that loved her; whereupon Andrew, perhaps without immediate answer more than a smile, would turn into his room, and reappear with what he had prepared for her to chew upon till they should meet again. Milton's sonnet, for instance, to the "virgin wise and pure,"[6] had long served her aspiration; equally wise and pure, Dawtie could understand it as well as she for whom it was written. To see the delight she took in it would have been a joy to any loving student of humanity. It had cost her more effort to learn than almost any song and perhaps, therefore, was the more precious. Andrew seldom gave her a book to learn from; in general he copied, in his clearest handwriting, whatever poem or paragraph he thought fit for Dawtie. When they next met, she would frequently repeat unasked what she had learned, and be rewarded with his unfailing look of satisfaction.

There was a secret between them—a secret proclaimed on the housetops, a secret hidden, the most precious of pearls, in their hearts—that the earth is the Lord's and the fullness thereof; that its work is the work of the Lord, whether the sowing of the field, the milking of the cow, the giving to the poor, the spending of wages, the reading of the Bible; that God is all in all, and every throb of gladness His gift; that their life came fresh every moment from His heart; that what was lacking to them would arrive the very moment He had made them ready for it. They were God's little ones in the world—nonetheless their own that they did not desire to swallow it or thrust it in their pockets. Among poverty-stricken Christians, consumed with care to keep ahold of the world and save their souls, they were as two children of the House. By living in the presence of the Living One, they had become themselves His presence—dim lanterns through which His light shone steady. Who obeys, shines.

Chapter 14.

SANDY AND GEORGE

Sandy had found it expedient to go to America, and had now been there twelve months. He had devised a machine of the value of which not even his patron could be convinced—he could not see the prospect of its making money fast enough to constitute a *good thing*. Sandy regarded it as a discovery, a revelation for the uplifting of a certain downtrodden portion of the community; and therefore, having saved a little money, had resolved to make it known in the States, where insight into probabilities is fresher. And now Andrew had a letter from him in which he mentioned that he had come across Mr. Crawford, already of high repute in Wall Street; that he had been kind to him, and having learned his object in visiting the country, and the approximate risk in bringing out his invention, had taken the thing into consideration. But the next mail brought another letter to the effect that, having learned the nature of the business done by Mr. Crawford, Sandy found himself unable to distinguish between it and gambling, or worse; it seemed to him a vortex whose very emptiness drew money into it. He had therefore drawn back, and declined to put the thing in Crawford's hands. This letter Andrew gave Dawtie to read, that she might see that Sandy remained a true man. He had never been anxious on the point, but was very glad that ignorance had not drawn his brother into evil connection.

Dawtie took the letter with her to read at her leisure. Unable, however, to understand something Sandy said concerning Mr.

Crawford's business, she asked a question or two of her mistress, which led to questions on Alexa's part. Finding out the subject of Sandy's letter, she wished to see it. Dawtie asked leave of Andrew, and gave it her.

Alexa read, and was both distressed and indignant, becoming at once George's partisan. Her distress diminished and her indignation increased as she reflected on the way which the unfavorable report reached her. The brothers were such peculiar men! She recalled the strange things she had heard of their childhood; doubtless their judgment was formed on an over-strained and quixotic idea of honesty! Besides, there had always been a strong socialistic tendency in them, which explained how Sandy could malign his benefactor! George was incapable of doing anything dishonorable, and so she would not trouble herself about it. But still, she would like to know how Andrew regarded the matter.

She asked him, therefore, what he thought of Sandy's procedure. Andrew replied that he did not know much about business, but that the only safety must lie in having nothing to do with what was doubtful; therefore Sandy had done right. Alexa said it was too bad of him to condemn where he confessed ignorance.

Andrew replied, "Ma'am, if Mr. Crawford is wrong, he is condemned; if he is right, my private doubt cannot hurt him. Sandy must act by his own doubt, not by Mr. Crawford's confidence."

Alexa grew more distressed, for she began to recall things George had said which she had not liked, but had succeeded in forgetting. If he had indeed gone astray, she hoped he would forget her; she could do without him! But the judgment of such a man as Sandy could settle nothing. Of humble origin and childish simplicity, he could not see the thing as a man of experience must! George might be all right, notwithstanding. At the same time, there was his father, whose reputation remained under a thick cloud, whose failed character rather than his ill-success had driven George to the other continent. Breed must mean something in a question of probabilities. It was the first time Alexa's thought had been turned into such a channel. She clung to the poor comfort that something must have passed at the interview so kindly sought by George, to set the quixotical young farmer against him. She would not utter his name to Andrew ever again!

She was right in thinking that George cherished a sincere affection for her. It was one of the spurs which drove him too eagerly after money. I doubt if any man starts with a developed love of money for its own sake—except, indeed, he be born of generations of Mammon worshipers. George had gone into speculation with the object of retrieving the position in which he had supposed himself born, and in the hope of winning the hand of his cousin—thinking too much of himself to offer what would not in the eye of the world be worth her acceptance. When he stepped on the inclined plane of dishonesty, he believed himself engaged only in legitimate speculation, but he was at once affected by the atmosphere about him. Wrapped in the breath of admiration and adulation surrounding men who cared for nothing but money-making, men who were not merely dishonest but the very serpents of dishonesty, against whom pickpockets will shine as angels of light; constantly under the softly persuasive influence of low morals and extravagant appreciation of cunning, he came by rapid degrees to think less and less of right and wrong. At first he called the doings of the place dishonest; then he called them sharp practice; then he called them a little shady; then, close sailing; then he said this or that transaction was deuced clever; then, that the man was more rogue than fool; then he laughed at the success of a vile trick; then he touched the pitch, and thinking all the time it was but with one finger, was presently besmeared all over—as was natural, for he who will touch is already smeared.

While Alexa was fighting his battles with herself, he had thrown down his arms in the only battle worth fighting. When he wrote to her, which he did regularly, he said no more about business than that his prospects were encouraging. How much his reticence may have had to do with a sense of her disapproval, it is difficult to tell.

Chapter 15.

MOTHER AND DAUGHTER

One lovely summer evening, Dawtie, with a bundle in her hand, looked from the top of a grassy knoll down onto her parents' turf cottage. The sun was setting behind her, and she looked as if she had just stepped from it as it touched the ground on which she stood, rosy with the rosiness of the sun but with a light in her countenance which came from a higher source, from the same nest as the sun himself. She paused but a moment, ran down the hill, and found her mother making the porridge. Mother and daughter neither embraced nor kissed nor even shook hands; but their faces glowed with delight, and words of joy and warmest welcome flowed between them.

"But ye havena lost yer place, have ye, hinny'?" said the mother.

"No, mother; there's no fear of that, as long's the laird or Miss Lexy's to the fore. They treat me—I willna say like one of themselves, but as if they would have liked me for one of themselves, if it had pleased the Lord to send me their way instead of yours. They're that good to me ye canna think!"

"Then what's brought ye the day?"

"I begged for a playday. I wanted to see An'rew."

"Eh, lass! I'm afraid for ye! Ye must not set your heart so high! An'rew's the best of men, but a lass canna have a man to herself just 'cause he's the best man in the world!"

"What mean ye by that, mother?" said Dawtie, looking a little scared. "Am I no to love An'rew, 'cause he's 'most as good's the

75

Lord would have him? Would ye have me hate him for it? Hasna he taught me to love God—to love Him better nor father, mother, An'rew, or anybody? I *will* love An'rew! What can ye mean, mother?"

"What I mean, Dawtie, is that ye mustna think because ye love him ye must have him; ye mustna think ye canna do wanting An'rew!"

"It's true, mother, I knowna what I should do wanting An'rew! Isna he always shoving the door of the kingdom a wee wider to let me see in the better? It's little marvel I love him! But as to wanting him for my own man, as ye have my father— mother, I would be ashamed of myself to think of any such thing! Clean affronted with myself, I would be!"

"Well, well, bairn! Ye was always a wiselike lass, and I must listen to ye! Only look to your heart."

"As for no loving him, mother—me that canna look at a blind kitten without loving it! Lo, mother! God made me so, an didna mean me no to love An'rew!"

"An'rew!" she repeated, as if the word meant the perfection of earth's worthiest, rendering the idea of appropriation too absurd.

Silence followed, but the mother was brooding.

"Ye must bethink ye, lass, how far he's above ye!" she said at length.

As the son of the farmer on whose land her husband was a cottar, Andrew seemed to her what the laird seemed to old John Ingram, and what the earl seemed to the laird, though the laird's family was ancient when the earl's had not been heard of. But Dawtie understood Andrew better than did her mother.

"You and me sees him far above, mother; but An'rew himself never thinks of no such things. He's so used to looking up, he's forgotten to look down. He holds his land from a higher than the laird, or the earl himself!"

The mother was silent. She was faithful and true; but, fed on the dried fish of logic and system and legalism, she could not follow the simplicities of her daughter's religion that trusted neither in notions about Him, nor even in what He had done, but in the live Christ Himself whom she loved and obeyed.

"If An'rew wanted to marry me," Dawtie went on, jealous for the divine liberty of her teacher, "which never came into 'is

76

head—na, no once—the same being taken up with far other things, it wouldna be because I was but a cotter lass that he wouldna take his own way! But the morn's the Sabbath day, and we'll have a walk together."

"I dinna altogether like these walks upon the Sabbath day," said the mother.

"Jesus walked on the Sabbath the same as any other day, mother!"

"Well, but He knew what He was about!"

"And so do I, mother! I know His will!"

"He had always something on hand fit to be done on the Sabbath!"

"And so have I the day, mother. If I was to do anything no fit in this His world, looking out of the eyes He gave me, with the hands and feet He gave me, I would just deserve to be nipped out at once, or sent into the outer darkness!"

"There's many must fare ill then, lass!"

"I'm saying only for myself. I know none so to blame as I would be myself."

"Isna that making yourself out better nor other folk, lass?"

"If I said I thought anything worth doing but the will of God, I would be a liar; if I say man or woman has nothing other to do in this world or the next, I say it believing each one of them must come to it at the long last. Few sees it yet, but the time's coming when each body will be as sure of it as I am. What wonder is't that I say't, with Jesus telling me the same from morning to night?"

"Lass, lass, I fear me, ye'll go out o' your mind!"

"It'll be into the mind of Christ, then, mother! I dinna care for my own mind. I have none of my own, and will stick to His. If I dinna make His mine, and stick to it, I'm lost! Now, mother, I'll set the things, and run over to the house, and let An'rew know I'm here."

"As ye will, lass. Ye're beyond me! I'll say nothing about willful women, for ye've been always a good daughter. I trust I have reason to hope the Lord willna be disappointed in ye."

Dawtie found Andrew in the stable, suppering his horses, told him she had something to talk to him about, and asked if he would let her go with him in his walk the next day. Andrew was delighted to see her, but he did not say so; and she was back home before her mother had taken the milk from the press.

In a few minutes her father appeared, and welcomed her with a sober joy. As they ate their supper, he could not help admiring her, she sat looking so well and nice and trim. He was a good-looking, workworn man, his hands absolutely callused with labor. But inside many such callused husks are ripening beautiful kingdom hands, for the time when "dear welcome Death" will loose and let us go from the graveclothes of the body that bind some of us even hand and foot. Rugged father and withered mother were beautiful in the eyes of Dawtie, and she and God saw them better than any other. Good, endless good, was on the way to them all! It was so pleasant to be waiting for the best of all good things.

Chapter 16.

ANDREW AND DAWTIE

Dawtie slept in peace and happy dreams till the next morning, when she was up almost with the sun and soon out in his low clear light. For the sun was strong again; the red labor and weariness were gone from his shining face. Everything about her seemed to know God, or at least to have had a moment's gaze upon Him. How else could everything look so content, hopeful, and happy? It is the man who will not fall in with the Father's bliss to whom the world seems soulless and dull. Dawtie was at peace because she desired nothing but what she knew He was best pleased to give her. Even had she cherished for Andrew the kind of love her mother feared, her Lord's will would have been her comfort and strength. If anyone says, "Then she could not know what love is!" I answer, "That person does not know what the better love is that lifts the being into such a serene air that it can fast from many things and yet be blessed beyond what any other granted desire could make it."

The scent of the sweet peas growing against the turf wall entered Dawtie's soul like a breath from the fields of heaven, where the children made merry with the angels, the merriest of playfellows, and where the winds and waters and all the living things were at their sportive call; where the little ones had babies to play with and did not hurt them, and where dolls were neither loved nor missed, being never thought of. Suchlike were the girl's imaginings as her thoughts went straying, inventing, discovering. She did not fear the Father would be angry with her for being His child and playing at creation. Who indeed but one in His loving heart can rightly love the making of the Maker?

When they had had their breakfast, and the old people were ready for church—where they would listen a little, sleep a little, sing heartily, and hear nothing to wake hunger, joy, or aspiration—Dawtie put a piece of oatcake in her pocket and went to join Andrew. She found him waiting, sprawled at his length in a bush of heather, with Henry Vaughn's *Silex Scintillan*[8], drawing from it "bright shoots of everlastingness" for his Sabbath day's delight. He read one and then another of the poems to Dawtie, who was pleased but not astonished. She was never astonished at anything; she had nothing in her to make anything beautiful by contrast; her mind was of beauty itself, and anything beautiful was to her but in the order and law of things—what was to be expected. Nothing struck her because of its rarity; the rare was at home in her country, and she was at home with it. When, for instance, he read from the section "Cock-Crowing,"

> "Father of lights! what sunny seed,
> what glance of day hast Thou confin'd
> into this bird?"

she took it up at once and understood it, felt that the good man had said the thing that was to be said, and loved him for it. She was not surprised to hear that the prayer was more than two hundred years old; were there not millions of years in front? Why should it be wonderful that a few years behind, men should have thought and felt as she did, and been able to say it as she never could! Had she not always loved the little cocks, and watched them learning to crow?

"But, An'rew," she said at length, "I want to tell ye something that's troubling me; then ye can learn me what ye like."

"Tell on, Dawtie," said Andrew.

"One night about a fortnight ago, I couldna sleep. I drove all the sheep I could gather in my brain, over one stile after another, but the sleep stuck to the wool of them, and each one took of it away with him. I wouldna have tried, but that I had to be up early and was feared I would sleep in.

"So I got up, and thought to sweep and dust the hall and the stairs; then if, when I lay down again, I should sleep too long, there would be a part of the day's work done! Ye know, An'rew, what the house is like; at the top of the stair that begins directly ye enter the house, there is a big irregular place, bigger than the floor of your barn, laid with flags. It is just as if all the different parts of the house had been built at different times round about it, and then it was itself roofed in by an after-thought. That's what we call the hall. The spare room opens on the left at the top of the stair, and to the right, across the hall, beyond the swell of the short thick tower ye see half of outside, is the door of the study. It is all round with books—some of them, mistress says, worth their weight in gold, they are so scarce. But the master trusts me to dust them. He used to do it himself, but now that he is getting old, he doesna like the trouble, and it makes him asthmatic. He says books need dusting more than anything else, but are in more danger of being hurt by it, and it makes him nervous to see me touch them. I have known him stand an hour watching me while I dusted, looking all the time as if he had just taken a dose of medicine. So I often do a few books at a time, as I can, when he isna in the way to be worried with it, though he always knows where I've been with my duster and my long-haired brush. And now it came across me that I had better dust some books first of all, as it was a good chance, he being sound asleep. So I lighted up my lamp, went straight to the study, and began where I last left off.

"As I was dusting, one of the books I came to looked so new and different from the rest that I opened it to see what it was like inside. It was full of pictures of mugs, and gold and silver jugs and cups—some of them plain and some colored; and one of the colored ones was so beautiful that I stood and looked at it. It was a gold cup, I suppose, for it was yellow; and all round the edge, and on the sides, it was set with stones, like the stones in mistress' rings, only much bigger. They were blue and red and green and yellow, and more colors than I can remember. The book said it was made by somebody, but I forget his name. It was a long name. The first part of it began with a *B*, and the second with a *C;* I remember that much. It was like *Benjamin*, but it wasna that. I put it back in its place, thinking I would ask

the master whether there really were such beautiful things, and
took down the next. Now whether that had been passed over
between the two batches, I dinna know, but it was so dusty that
before I would touch another I gave the duster a shake, and the
wind of it blew the lamp out. I took it up to carry it to the
kitchen and kindle it again when, to my astonishment, I saw a
light under the door of a press which was always locked, and
where master said he kept his most precious books. 'How
strange!' I thought. 'A light inside a locked cupboard!'

"Then I remembered how in one place where I had been,
there was, in a room over the stable, a press whose door had no
fastening except a bolt on the inside, which set me thinking,
and some terrible things came to me that made me remember
it. So now I said to myself, 'There's someone in there, after the
master's books!' It was not a likely thing, but the night is the
time for fancies, and in the night you dinna know what is likely
and what isna. One thing, however, was clear—I ought to find
out what the light meant. Fearful things darted one after another through my head as I went to the door, but there was one
thing I daredna do, and that was to leave it unopened. So I
opened it as softly as I could, in terror lest the thief should hear
my heart beating. When I could peep in, what do you think I
saw? I couldna believe my eyes! There was a great big room! I
rubbed my eyes and stared, and rubbed them again and
stared—thinking to rub it away. But there it was, a big, odd-
shaped room, part of it with round sides, and in the middle of
the room a table, and on the table a burning lamp, and master
at the table with his back to me! I was so astonished that I
forgot I had no business there and ought to go away. I stood
like an idiot, amazed and lost.

"And willna you wonder when I tell you that the laird was
holding up to the light, between his two hands, the very cup I
had been looking at in the book, the stones of it flashing all the
colors of the rainbow! I should think it a dream, if I didna
know it was not. I dinna believe I made any noise, for I couldna
move, but he started up with a cry to God to preserve him, set
the cup on the table, threw something over it, caught up a
wicked-looking knife, and turned round. His face was like that
of a corpse, and I could see him tremble. I stood steady, for it
wasna time to turn away! I supposed he expected to see a rob-

ber, and would be glad when he discovered it was only me; but when he did, his fear changed to anger, and he came at me. His eyes were flaming, and he looked as if he would kill me. I wasna frightened—poor old man, I was able for him any day—but I was afraid of hurting him. So I closed the door quickly, and went softly to my own room, where I stood a long time in the dark, listening, but heard nothing more. What am I to do, An'rew?"

"I don't know that you have to do anything. You have one thing not to do—that is, to tell anybody what you have seen."

"I was forced to tell you because I didna know what to do. It makes me *so* sorry!"

"It was no fault of yours! You acted to the best of your knowledge, and could not help what came of it. Perhaps nothing more will come. Leave the thing alone, and if he says anything, tell him how it happened."

"But, An'rew, I dinna think you see what it is that troubles me! I am afraid my master is a miser! The mistress and he take their meals, like poor people, in the kitchen! The room where he was must be the dining room of the house! And though my eyes were tethered to the flashing cup, I couldna help seeing it was full of strange beautiful things, and the armor of knights, when they fought on their horses' backs. Before people had money, they must have misered other things! Some girls miser their clothes, and never go decent!"

"Suppose him a miser," said Andrew. "What could you do? How are you to help it?"

"That's what I want to know! I love my master, and there must be a way to help it! It was terrible to see him, in the middle of the night, gazing at that cup as if he had found the most precious thing that can ever have existed on the earth! Poor man! He looked at the cup as you might at a manuscript! His soul was at it feasting upon it! Now wasna that miserly?"

"It was like it!"

"And I love my master!" repeated Dawtie, thus putting afresh the question what she was to do.

"Why do you love him, Dawtie?" asked Andrew.

"Because I'm set to love him. Besides, we're told to love our enemies; then surely we're to love our friends! He has always been a friend to me! He never said a hard word to me, even when I was handling his books. He trusts me with them! I canna help loving him—a good deal, An'rew! And it's what I've got to do!"

"There's not a doubt about it, Dawtie. You've got to love him, and you do love him!"

"But there's more than that, An'rew! To hear the laird talk, you would think he cared more for the Bible than for the whole world—not to say gold cups! He talks of the merits of the Saviour, that you would think he loved Him with all his heart! But I canna get it out of my mind, ever since I saw that look on his face, that he *loves* that cup—that it's his graven image, his idol! How else should he get up in the middle of the night to—to—well, it was just like worshiping it!"

"You're afraid then that he's a hypocrite, Dawtie?"

"No, I darena think that—if it were only for fear I should stop loving him—and that would be as bad! For isna it as bad not to love a human being, as it would be to love a thing?"

"Perhaps worse," said Andrew.

"Something must be done!" she went on. "He canna be left like that! But if he has any love to his Master, how is it that the love of that Master hasna cast out the love of Mammon? I canna understand it."

"You have asked a hard question, Dawtie! But a cure may be going on, and yet take a thousand years or ages to work it out!"

"What if it shouldna be begun yet!"

"That would be terrible!"

"What then am I to do, An'rew? You always say we must do something! You say there is no faith but what does something!"

"The Apostle James said so, a few years before I was born, Dawtie!"

"Dinna make fun of me, please, An'rew! I like it, but I canna bear it today, my head is so full of the poor old laird."

"Make fun of you, Dawtie? Never! But I don't know yet how to answer you."

"Well, then, what am I to do?" persisted Dawtie.

"Wait, of course, till you know what to do. When you don't know what to do, don't do anything—only keep asking the Thinker of wisdom. And until you know, don't let the laird see that you know anything."

With this answer Dawtie was content, and they turned to go home.

Chapter 17.

DAWTIE AND THE CUP

The old laird had a noteworthy mental fabric. Believing himself a true lover of literature, and especially of poetry, he would lecture for ten minutes on the right mode of reading a verse in Milton or Dante; but as to Satan[9] or Beatrice[10], he would pin his faith to the majority of the commentators—Milton's Satan was too noble, and Beatrice was no woman, but theology. He was discriminative to a degree altogether admirable as to the rightness or wrongness of a proposition with regard to conduct, but owed his respectability to good impulses without any effort of the will. He was almost as orthodox as Paul before his conversion, lacking only the heart and the courage to persecute.

Whatever the eternal wisdom saw in him, the thing most present to his own consciousness was the love of rare historic relics. And this love was so mingled in warp and woof, that he did not know whether a thing was more precious to him for its rarity, its money value, or its historic and reliquary interest. All the time he was a schoolmaster, he had saved every possible halfpenny to buy books, not because of their worth or human interest, but because of their literary fame or the scarcity of the edition. In the holidays he would go about questing for the prey that his soul loved, hunting after precious things; but not even the precious things of the everlasting hills would be precious to him until they had received the stamp of curiosity. His life consisted of a continual search for something new that was known as known of old.

It had hardly yet occurred to him that he must one day leave his things and exist without them, no longer to brood over them, take them in his hands, turn, stroke, and admire them. Yet, strange to say, he would at times anxiously seek to satisfy himself that he was safe for "a better world," as he called it, to feel certain that his faith was of the sort he supposed intended by Paul—not that he had himself gathered anything from the apostle, but all from the tradition of his church concerning the teaching of the apostle. He was anxious as to his safety for the world to come; and yet, while his dearest joy lay treasured in that hidden room, he never thought of the hour when he must leave it all, and go houseless and pocketless and empty-handed, if not armless, in the wide, closetless space, hearing ever in the winds and the rain and the sound of the seawaves the one question, "Whose shall those things be which thou hast provided?" Like the rich man to whom God said the words, he had gathered much goods for many years—hundreds and hundreds of things, every one of which he knew, and every one of which he loved.

A new scratch on the bright steel of one of his suits of armor was a scratch on his heart; the moth and the rust troubled him sore, for he could not keep them away; and where his treasure was, there was his heart, devoured by the same moth, consumed by the same rust. He had much suffering from his possessions and was more exposed to misery than the miser of gold; for the hoarded coin of the latter may indeed be stolen, but he fears neither moth nor rust nor scratch nor decay. The laird cherished his things as no mother her little ones. Nearly sixty years he had been gathering them, and their money worth was great, but he had no idea of its amount, for he could not have endured the exposure and handling of them which a valuation must involve.

His love for his books had somewhat declined in the growth of his love for things, and now, by degrees not very slow, his love of things was graduating itself after what he supposed their money value. His soul not only clave to the dust, but was going deeper and deeper in the dust as it wallowed. All day long he was living in the past and growing old. It is one thing to grow old in the past, and another to grow old in the present! As he took his walk about his farms, or sat at his meals, or held a

mild, soulless conversation with his daughter, his heart was
growing old, not healthily in the present, which is to ripen, but
unwholesomely in the past, which is to consume with a dry rot.
While he read the Bible at prayers, trying hard to banish world-
ly things from his mind, his thoughts were not in the story or
the argument he read, but hovering, like a bird over its nest,
about the darlings of his heart. Yea, even while he prayed, his
soul, instead of casting off the clay of the world, was loaded and
dragged down with all the still-moldering, slow-changing things
that lined the walls and filled the drawers and cabinets of his
treasure chamber. It was a place whose existence not even his
daughter knew; for before ever she entered the house, he had
taken with him a mason from the town, and built up the entrance to it from the hall, ever afterward keeping the other
door of it that opened from his study carefully locked, and
leaving it to be regarded as the door of a closet.

It was as terrible as Dawtie felt it, that a live human soul
should thus haunt the sepulcher of the past, and love the life-
less, turning a room hitherto devoted to hospitality and mirth-
ful relations into the temple of his selfish idolatry. It was as one
of the rooms carved for the dead in the *Beban El Malook*. Surely,
if left to himself, the ghost that loved it would haunt the place!
But he could not surely be permitted, for it might postpone a
thousand years his discovery of the emptiness of a universe of
such treasures. No, he was moldering into the world of spirits
in the heart of an avalanche of the dust of ages, dust material
from his hoards, dust moral and spiritual from his withering
soul itself.

The next day he was ill, which, common as is illness to humanity, was strange, for it had never befallen him before. He
was unable to leave his bed. But he never said a word to his
daughter, who alone waited on him, as to what had happened
in the night. He had passed it sleepless, and without the possibility of a dream on which to fall back; yet, when morning
came, he was in much doubt whether what he had seen—namely, the face of Dawtie, peeping in at the door—was a reality, or
but a vision of the night. For when he opened the door which
she had closed, all was dark, and not the slightest sound
reached his quick ear from the swift foot of her retreat. He
turned the key twice, and pushed two bolts, eager to regard the

vision as a providential rebuke of his carelessness in leaving the door on the latch—for the first time, he imagined. Then he tottered back to his chair, and sank on it in a cold sweat. For, while the confidence grew that what he had seen was but "a false creation proceeding from the heat-oppressed brain," it was far from comfortable to feel that he could no longer depend upon his brain to tell him only the thing that was true. What if he were going out of his mind, on the way to encounter a succession of visions—without reality, but possessed of its power? What if they should be such whose terror would compel him to disclose what most he desired to keep covered? How fearful to be no more his own master, but at the beck and call of a disordered brain, a maniac king in a *cosmos acosmos!*

Better it *had been* Dawtie, and she *had seen* in his hands Benvenuto Cellini's[11] chalice made for Pope Clement the Seventh[12] to drink the holy wine—worth thousands of pounds! Perhaps she had seen it! No, surely she had not! He must be careful not to make her suspect. He would watch her and say nothing.

But Dawtie, conscious of no wrong and full of love to the old man, showed an untroubled face when next she met him; and he made up his mind that he would rather have her ignorant. Thenceforward, naturally though childishly, he was even friendlier to her than before; it was so great a relief to find that he had not to fear her!

The next time Dawtie was dusting his books, she felt strongly drawn to look again at the picture of the cup, for it seemed now to hold in it a human life! She took down the book, and began where she stood to read what it said about the chalice, referring as she read from letterpress to drawing. It was taken from an illumination in a missal, printed in a place where the cup was known to have been copied; and it rendered the description in the letterpress unnecessary except in regard to the stones and hammered reliefs on the hidden side. She quickly learned the names of the gems, that she might see how many were in the high priest's breastplate and the gates of the New Jerusalem, then proceeded to the history of the chalice. She read that it had come into the possession of Cardinal York[13], the brother of Charles Edward Stuart[14], and had been by him entrusted to his sister-in-law, the Duchess of Albany[15], from whose house it had disappeared, some said stolen, others said sold. It came next to the historic surface in the possession of a certain earl whose love of curiosities was well known; but from his collection again it vanished, this time beyond a doubt stolen, probably years before it was missed.

A new train of thought was presently in motion in the mind of the girl—*the beautiful cup was stolen! It was not where it ought to be! It was not at home. It was a captive, a slave!*

She lowered the half-closed book with a finger between the leaves, and stood thinking. She did not for a moment believe her master had stolen it, though the fear had flashed through her mind. It had been stolen and sold, and he had bought it at length from someone whose possession of it was nowise suspicious! But he must know now that it had been stolen, for here with the cup was the book which said so! That would be nothing if the rightful owner were not known; but he was known, and the thing ought to be his! The laird might not be bound, she was not sure, to restore it at his own loss, if when he bought it he was not aware that it was stolen; but he was bound to restore it at the price he had paid for it, if the former owner would give it. This was bare justice, and mere righteousness! No theft could make the owner not the rightful owner, though other claims upon the thing might come in! One ought not to be enriched by another's misfortune!

Dawtie was sure that a noble of the kingdom of heaven would not wait for the money, but would with delight send the cup where it ought to have been all the time. She knew better, however, than to require magnificence in any shape from the poor wizened soul of her master—a man who knew all about everything, and whom yet she could not but fear to be nothing; as Dawtie had learned to understand life, the laird did not yet exist. But he well knew right from wrong; therefore the discovery she just made affected her duty toward him. It might be impossible to make impression on the miserliness of a miser, but upon the honesty in a miser it might be possible! The goblet was not his!

But the love of things dulls the conscience; and he might not be able, having bought and paid for it, to see that the thing was not therefore *his*. He might defend himself from seeing it! To Dawtie, this made the horror of his condition the darker. She was one of God's babes, who cannot help seeing the true state of things. Logic was to her but the smoke that rises from the burning truth; she saw what is altogether above and beyond logic—the right thing, whose meanest servant is logic—the hewer of its wood, not the drawer of its water; the merest scullion and sweeper away of lies from the pavement of its courts.

With a sigh she woke to the knowledge that she was not doing her work, and rousing herself, was about to put the book on its shelf. But, her finger being still in the place, she would have one more glance at the picture! To her dismay she saw that she had made a mark on the plate, and of the enormity of making a dirty mark on a book, her master had made her well aware.

She was in great distress. What was to be done? She did not once think of putting it away and saying nothing. To have reasoned that her master would never know would have been an argument, pressing and imperative, for informing him at once. She had done him an injury, and the injury must be confessed and lamented; it was all that was left to be done! "Such a mischance!" she said, then bethought herself that there was no such thing as mischance, when immediately it flashed upon her that here was the door open for the doing of what was required of her. She was bound to confess the wrong, and that would lead in the disclosure of what she knew, rendering it comparatively easy to use some remonstrance with the laird, whom she saw in her mind's eye like a beggarman tottering down a steep road to a sudden precipice. Her duty was now so plain that she felt no desire to consult Andrew. She was not one to ask an opinion for the sake of talking; she went to Andrew only when she wanted light to do the right thing. When the light was around her, she knew how to walk and troubled no one.

At once she laid down the book and duster, and went to find the laird. But he had slipped away to the town, to have a rummage in a certain little shop in a back street, which he had not rummaged for a time long enough, he thought, to have let something come in. It was no relief to Dawtie; the thing would be all the day before her instead of behind her! It burned within her, not like a sin but like what it was, a confession unconfessed. Little wrong as she had done, Dawtie was yet

familiar with the lovely potency of confession to annihilate it.
She knew it was the turning from wrong that killed it, that
confession gave the *coup de grace* to offense. She dreaded not a
little the displeasure of her master, and yet dreaded still more
his distress.

She prepared the laird's supper with a strange mingling of
hope and anxiety—she feared having to go to bed without telling him. But he came at last, almost merry, with a brown paper
parcel under his arm, over which he was very careful. Poor
man, he little knew there waited him at the moment a demand
from the eternal justice, almost as terrible as, "This night they
require thy soul of thee!" (What a *they* is that! Who are *they*?)
The torture of the moral rack was ready for him at the hands of
his innocent housemaid! In no way can one torture another
more than by waking conscience against love, passion, or pride.

He laid his little parcel carefully on the supper table, said
rather a shorter grace than usual, began to eat his porridge,
praised it as very good, spoke of his journey and whom he had
seen, and was more talkative than his wont. He informed Alexa,
almost with jubilation, that he had at length found an old book
he had been long on the watch for—a book that treated, in
ancient broad Scots, of the laws of verse, in a full, even exhaus-
tive manner. He pulled it from his pocket.

"It is worth at least ten times what I gave for it!" he said.

Dawtie wondered whether there ought to have been some
division of the difference, but she was aware of no call to speak.
One thing was enough for one night!

Then came prayers. The old man read how David deceived
the Philistines, telling them a falsehood as to his raids. He read
the narrative with a solemnity of tone that would have graced
the most righteous action; was it not the deed of a man according to God's own heart? How could it be other than right!
Casuist[16] ten times a week, he did not question the righteousness of David's wickedness! Then he prayed, giving thanks for
the mercy that had surrounded them all the day, shielding
them from the danger and death which lurked for them in
every corner. Dawtie wondered what he would say when death
did get him. Would he thank God then? And when she spoke to
him, would he see that God wanted to deliver him from a worse
danger than any out-of-doors? Would he see that it was from

much mercy he was made more uncomfortable than perhaps ever before in his life?

At length his offering was completed—how far accepted, who can tell? He was God's, and He who gave him being would be his Father to the full possibility of God. They rose from their knees; the laird took up his parcel and book, and his daughter went with him.

Chapter 18.

DAWTIE AND
THE LAIRD

As soon as Dawtie heard her mistress' door close, she followed her
master to the study, and arrived just as the door of the hidden
room was being shut behind him. There was not a moment to
be lost! She went straight to it, and knocked rather loudly. No
answer came. She knocked again. Still there was no answer. She
knocked a third time, and after a little fumbling with the lock,
the door opened a chink, and a ghastly face, bedewed with
drops of terror, peeped through. She was standing a little back,
and his eyes did not at once find the object they sought; then
suddenly they lighted on her, and the laird shook from head to
foot.

"What is it, Dawtie?" he faltered out in a broken voice.

"Please, sir," answered Dawtie, "I have something to confess;
would ye hearken to me?"

"No, no, Dawtie! I am sure you have nothing to confess!"
returned the old man, eager to send her away, and to prevent
her from seeing the importance of the room whose entrance
she had discovered. "Or," he went on, finding she did not
move, "if you have done anything, Dawtie, that you ought not
to have done, confess it to God. It is to Him you must confess,
not to a poor mortal like me! For my part, if it lies to me, I
forgive you, and there is an end! Go to your bed, Dawtie."

"Please, sir, I canna. If ye willna hear me, I'll sit down at the
door of this room, and sit till—"

"What room, Dawtie? Call you this a room? It's a wee bit

93

closet where I say my prayers before I go to bed."

But as he spoke, his blood ran cold within him, for he had uttered a deliberate lie—two lies in one breath. The "bit closet" was the largest room in the house, and he had never prayed a prayer in it since first he entered it! He was unspeakably distressed at what he had done, for he had always cherished the idea that he was one who would not lie to save his life. And now in his old age he had lied, who when a boy had honor enough to keep from lying! Worst of all, now that he had lied, he must hold to the lie! He *dared* not confess it! He stood sick and trembling.

"I'll wait, sir," said Dawtie, distressed at his suffering, and more distressed that he could lie who never forgot his prayers! Alas, he was farther down the wrong road than she had supposed!

Ashamed for his sake, and also for her own, to look him in the face—for he imagined she believed him, while she knew that he lied—she turned her back on him. He caught at his advantage, glided out, and closed the door behind him. When Dawtie again turned, she saw him in her power.

Her trial was come; she had to speak for life or death! But she remembered that the Lord told His disciples to take no care how they should speak, for when the time came it would be given them to speak. So she began by simply laying down the thing that was in her hand.

"Sir," she said, "I am very sorry, but this morning I made a dirty mark in one of your books!"

Her words alarmed him a little, and made him forget for the instant his more important fears. But he took care to be gentle with her; it would not do to offend her! For was she not aware that where they stood was a door by which he went in and out!

"You make me uneasy, Dawtie!" he said. "What book was it? Let me see it."

"I will, sir."

She turned to take it down, but the laird followed her saying, "Point it out to me, Dawtie. I will get it."

She did so. It opened at the plate.

"There is the mark!" she said. "I am right sorry."

"So am I!" returned the laird. "But," he added, willing she should feel his clemency, and knowing the book was not a rare

94

one, "it is a book still, and you will be more careful another time! For you must remember, Dawtie, that you don't come into this room to read the books, but to dust them. You can go to bed now with an easy mind, I hope!"

Dawtie was so touched by the kindness and forbearance of her master, that the tears rose in her eyes, and she felt strengthened for her task. What would she not have encountered for his deliverance!

"Please, sir," she said, "let me show you a thing you never perhaps happened to read!" And taking the book from his hand—he was too much astonished to retain it—she turned over the engraving, and showed him the passage which stated that the cup had disappeared from the possession of its owner, and had certainly been stolen.

Finding he said not a word, she ventured to lift her eyes to his, and saw again the corpselike face that had looked through the chink in the door.

"What do you mean?" he stammered. "I do not understand." His lips trembled, and she wondered if it was possible that he had had to do with the stealing of it.

The truth was this: he had learned the existence of the cup from this very book, and had never rested until, after a search of more than ten years, he at length found it in the hands of a poor man who dared not offer it publicly for sale. Once in the laird's possession, the thought of giving it up, or of letting the owner redeem it, had never even occurred to him. Yet the treasure made him rejoice with a trembling which all his casuistry would have found it hard to explain; for he would not confess to himself its real cause—namely, that his God-born essence was uneasy with a vague knowledge that it lay in the bosom of a thief.

"Dinna ye think, sir," said Dawtie, "that whoever has that cup ought to send it back to the place it was stolen from?"

Had the old man been a developed hypocrite, he would have replied at once, "He certainly ought." But by word of mouth to condemn himself would have been to acknowledge to himself that he ought to send the cup home, and this he dared not do. Men who will not do as they know, make strange confusion in themselves. The worst rancor in the vessel of peace is the consciousness of wrong in a not-all-unrighteous soul. The laird was false to his own self; but to confess himself false would be to initiate a change which would render life worthless to him! What would all his fine things be without their heart of preciousness, the one jewel that now was nowhere in the world but in his house, in the secret chamber of his treasures, which would be a rifled case without it! As is natural to one who will not do right, he began to argue the moral question, treating as a point of casuistry that which troubled the mind of the girl.

"I don't know, Dawtie!" he said. "It is not likely that the person that has the cup, whoever he may be—that is, if the cup be still in existence—is the same who stole it; and it would hardly be justice to punish the innocent for the guilty—as would be the case, if, supposing I had bought the cup, I had to lose the money I paid for it. Should the man who had not taken care of the cup, have his fault condoned at my expense? Did he not deserve, the man might say, to be so punished, placing huge temptation in the path of the needy, to the loss of their precious souls, and letting a priceless thing go loose in the world, to work ruin to whoever might innocently buy it?"

His logic did not serve to show him the falsehood of his reasoning, for his heart was in the lie. "Ought I or he," he went on, "to be punished because he kept the thing ill? And how far would the quixotic obligation descend? A score of righteous men may by this time have bought and sold the cup! Is it some demon talisman, that the last must meet the penalty, when the original owner, or some descendant of the man who lost it, chooses to claim it? For anything we know, he may himself have pocketed the price of the rumored theft! Can you not see it would be flagrant injustice, fit indeed to put an end to all buying and selling! It would annihilate transfer of property! Possession would mean only strength to keep, and the world would fall into confusion."

"It would be hard, I grant," confessed Dawtie, "but the man who has it ought at least to give the head of the family, in which it had been, the chance of buying it back at the price it cost him. If he could not buy it back—then the thing would have to be thought over."

"I confess I don't see the thing," returned the laird. "But the question needs not keep you out of bed, Dawtie! It is not often a girl in your position takes an interest in the abstract. Besides," he resumed, another argument occurring to him, "a thing of such historical value and interest ought to be where it is cared for, not where it is in danger every moment."

"There might be something in that," allowed Dawtie, "if it was where everybody could see it. But where is the good if it be but for the eyes of one man!"

The eyes she met fixed themselves upon her till their gaze grew to a stony stare. She *must* know that he had it! Or did she only suspect? He must not commit himself. He must set a watch on the door of his lips! What an uncomfortable girl to have in the house. Oh those self-righteous Ingrams! What mischief they did! His impulse was to dart into his treasure cave, lock himself in, and hug the radiant chalice. He dared not. He must endure instead the fastidious conscience and probing tongue of an intrusive maidservant!

"But," he rejoined, with an attempt at a smile, "if the pleasure the one man took in it should, as is easy to imagine, exceed immeasurably the aggregate pleasure of the thousands who would look upon it and pass it by—what then?"

"The man would enjoy it the more that many saw it—except he loved it for greed, when he would be rejoicing in iniquity, for the cup would not be his. And anyhow, he could not take it with him when he died!"

The face of the miser grew grayer, his lip trembled, but he said nothing. He was beginning to hate Dawtie! She was an enemy! She sought his discomfiture, his misery! He had read strange things in certain old books, and half believed some of them. What if Dawtie was one of those evil powers in pleasant shape that haunt a man, learn the secrets of his heart, and gain influence over him that they may tempt him to yield his soul to the enemy? She was set on ruining him! Certainly she knew the cup was in his possession! He must temporize! He must *seem* to listen. But as soon as fit reason could be found, such as would neither compromise him nor offend her, she must be sent away! And, of all things, she must not gain the means of proving what she now perhaps only suspected, and was seeking assurance of! He stood thinking. It was but for a moment; for the very next words from the lips of the girl that was to him little more than a housebroom, set him face-to-face with reality—the one terror of the unreal.

"Eh, master, sir," said Dawtie with the tears in her eyes, "dinna ye *know* that ye *have* to give the man that owns that golden bowl the chance of buying it back?"

The laird shivered. He dared not ask, "How do you know?" for he dared not hear the thing proved to him. If she did know, he would not front her proof! He would not have her even suppose it an acknowledged fact!

"If I had the cup," he began, but she interrupted him, for it was time they should have done with lying.

"Ye know ye have the cup, sir!" she said. "And I know too, for I saw it in yer hands!"

"You shameless, prying hussy!" he began, in a rage at last, but the eager tearful earnestness of her face made him bethink himself. It would not do to make an enemy of her! "Tell me, Dawtie," he said, with sudden change of tone, "how is it you came to see it."

She told him all—how and when; and he knew that he had seen her see him.

He managed to give a poor little laugh.

"All is not gold that glitters, Dawtie!" he said. "The cup you saw was not the one in the book, but an imitation of it—mere gilded tin and colored glass—copied from the picture, as near as they could make it—just to see better what it must have been like. Why, my good girl, that cup would be worth thousands of pounds! So go to bed, and don't trouble yourself about gold cups. It is not likely any of them will come our way."

Simple as Dawtie was, she did not believe him. But she saw no good to be done by disputing what he ought to know.

"It wasna about the gold cup I was troubling myself!" she said, hesitatingly.

"You are right there!" he replied, with another deathly laugh. "It was not! But you have been troubling me about nothing half the night, and I am shivering with cold! We really must, both of us, go to bed! What would your mistress say!"

"No," persisted Dawtie, "it wasna about the cup, gold or no gold; it was and is about my master I'm troubled! I'm terrible afraid for ye, sir! Ye're a worshiper of Mammon, sir!"

The laird laughed, for the danger was over! To Dawtie's deep dismay he laughed.

"My poor girl," he said, "you take an innocent love of curious

98

things for the worship of Mammon! Don't imagine me jesting. How could you believe an old man like me, an elder of the kirk, a dispenser of her sacred things, guilty of the awful crime of Mammon-worship?"

He imagined her ignorantly associating the idea of some idolatrous ritual with what to him was but a phrase—the worship of Mammon. "Do you not remember the words of Christ," he continued, "that a man *cannot* serve God and Mammon? If I be a Christian, as you will hardly doubt, it follows that I am not a worshiper of Mammon, for the two cannot go together."

"But that's just the question, sir! A man who worships God worships Him with his whole heart and soul and strength and mind. If he wakes at night, it is to worship God; if he is glad in his heart, it is because God is, and one day he shall behold His face in brightness. If a man worships God, he loves Him so that no love can come between him and God; if the earth was removed, and the mountains cast into the midst of the sea, it would be all one to him, for God would be all the same. Isna it so, sir?"

"You are a good girl, Dawtie, and I approve of every word you say. It would more than savor of presumption to profess that I loved God up to the point you speak of; but I deserve to love Him. Doubtless a man ought to love God so, and we are all sinners just because we do not love God so. But we have the atonement!"

"But sir," answered Dawtie, the silent tears running down her face, "I love God that way! I dinna care a dust for anything without Him! When I go to bed, I dinna care if I never wake again in this world; I shall be where He would have me!"

"You presume, Dawtie! I fear me much you presume! What if that shall be in hell?"

"If it be, it will be the best. It will be to set me right. O sir, He is so good! Tell me one thing, sir. When you die—"

"Tut, tut, lass! There's no occasion to think about that yet awhile! We're in the hands of a reconciled God!"

"What I want to know," pursued Dawtie, "is how you will feel, how you will get on, when you haven't got anything!"

"Not anything, girl? Are you losing your senses? Of course we shall want nothing then! I shall have to talk to the doctor about you! We shall have you killing us in our beds to know how we like it!"

He laughed, but it was a rather scared laugh.

"What I mean is," she persisted, "when you have no body, and no hands to take hold of your cup, what will you do without it?"

"What if I leave it to you, Dawtie?" returned the laird, with a stupid mixture of joke and avarice in his cold eye.

"Please, sir, I didna ask what would you do with it, but what would you do without it, when it willna come either out of your heart nor into your hands! It must be misery to a miser to have nothing!"

"A miser, hussy!"

"A lover of things, more than a lover of God!"

"Well, perhaps you have the better of me!" he said, after a cowed pause, for he perceived there was no compromise possible with Dawtie: she knew perfectly what she meant, and he could neither escape her logic, nor change her determination, whatever that might be. "I daresay you are right! I will think what ought to be done about that cup!"

He stopped, self-amazed—he had committed himself, as much as confessed the cup genuine! But Dawtie had not been deceived, and had not been thinking about the cup. Only it was plain that if he would consent to part with it for its worth, that would be a grand beginning toward the renouncing of dead things altogether, toward the turning to the Living One the love that now gathered, clinging and haunting, about gold cups and graved armor, and suchlike vapors and vanishings that pass with the sunsets and the snows. She fell on her knees and, in the spirit of a child and of the Apostle of the Gentiles, she cried, laying her little red hands together and uplifting them to her master in purest entreaty.

"O laird, laird, ye've been good and kind to me, and I love ye, the Lord knows! I pray ye, for Christ's sake be reconciled to God, for ye have been serving Mammon and no Him, and ye have just said we canna serve the two, and what'll come of it God only can tell, but it *must* be misery!"

Words failed her. She rose, and left the room, with her apron to her eyes.

The laird stood a moment or two like one lost, then went hurriedly into his "closet" and shut the door. Whether he went on his knees to God as did Dawtie to him, or began again to gloat over his Cellini goblet, I do not know.

Dawtie cried herself to sleep, and came down in the morning very pale. Her duty had left her exhausted, and with a kind of nausea toward all the ornaments and books in the house. A cock crew loud under the window of the kitchen. She dropped on her knees, said, "Father of Lights!" and not a word beside, rose and began to rouse the fire.

When breakfast time came and the laird appeared, he looked much as usual, only a little weary, which his daughter set down to his journey the day before. He revived, however, as soon as he had succeeded in satisfying himself that Alexa knew nothing of what had passed. How staid, discreet, and compact of common sense, Alexa seemed to him beside Dawtie, whose want of education left her mind a waste swamp for the vagaries of whatever will-o'-the-wisp an overstrained religious fantasy might generate! But however much the laird might look the same as before, he could never be again as he had been, knowing that Dawtie knew what she knew.

"You'll do a few of the books today, won't you, Dawtie," he said, "when you have time? I never thought I should trust anyone! I would sooner have old Meg shave me than let her dust an Elzevir!"[17] Ha! Ha! Ha!"

Dawtie was glad that at least he left the door open between them. She said she would do a little dusting in the afternoon, and would be very careful. Then the laird rose and went out; and Dawtie perceived, with a shoot of compassion mingled with a mild remorse, that he had left his breakfast almost untasted.

But after that, so far from ever beginning any sort of conversation with her, he seemed uncomfortable the moment they happened to be alone together. If he caught her eye, he would say hurriedly, and as if acknowledging a secret between them, "By and by, Dawtie!" or, "I'm thinking about the business, Dawtie!" or, "I'm making up my mind, Dawtie!" and so leave her. On one occasion he said, "Perhaps you will be surprised someday, Dawtie!"

On her part Dawtie never felt that she had any more to say to him. She feared at times that she had done him evil rather than good, by pressing upon him a duty she had not persuaded him to perform. She spoke of this fear to Andrew, but he answered decisively, "If you believed you ought to speak to him, and have discovered in yourself no wrong motive, you must not trouble yourself about the result. That may be a thousand years off yet. You may have sent him into a hotter purgatory, and at the same time made it shorter for him. We know nothing but that God is righteous."

Dawtie was comforted, and things went on as before. Where people know their work and do it, life has few blank spaces for boredom, and they are seldom to be pitied. Where people have not yet found their work, they may be more to be pitied than those that beg their bread. When a man knows his work but will not do it, pity him more than one who is to be hanged tomorrow.

Chapter 19.

ANDREW AND ALEXA

Andrew had occasion to call on the laird to pay his father's rent; and Alexa, who had not seen him for some time, thought him improved both in carriage and speech, and wondered. She did not take into account his relations with God, or with highest human minds in his reading, and his constant wakefulness to carry into action what things he learned. Thus trained in noblest fashions of freedom, it was small wonder that his bearing and manners, the natural outcome and expression of his habits of being, should grow in liberty. There was in them the change only of development. By the side of such education as this, dealing with reality and inborn dignity, what mattered any amount of ignorance as to social custom? Society may judge its own; this man was not of it, and as much surpassed its most accomplished pupils in all the essentials of breeding as the Apostle Paul was a better gentleman than any man who has merely mastered his manners. The training may be slow, but it is perfect. To him who has yielded self, all things are possible. Andrew was aware of no difference. He seemed to himself the same as when a boy.

Alexa had not again alluded to his brother's letter concerning George Crawford, fearing he might say what she would find unpleasant. But now she wanted to get a definite opinion from him in regard to certain modes of money-making, which had naturally of late occupied a good deal of her thought.

"What is your notion concerning money-lending—I mean at interest, Mr. Ingram?" she said. "I hear it is objected to nowadays by some that set up for teachers!"

"It is by no means the first time in the world's history," answered Andrew.

"I want to know what you think of it, Mr. Ingram."

"I know little," replied Andrew, "of any matter with which I have not had to deal practically."

"But ought not one to have his ideas ready for the time when he will have to deal practically?" said Alexa.

"Mine would be pretty sure to be wrong," answered Andrew, "and there is no time to spend in gathering wrong ideas and then changing them!"

"On the contrary, they would be less warped by personal interest."

"Could circumstances arise in which it would not be my first interest to be honest?" said Andrew. "Would not my judgment be quickened by the compulsion and the danger? In no danger myself, might I not judge too leniently of things from which I should myself recoil? Selfishly smoother with regard to others because less anxious about their honesty than my own, might I not yield them what, were I in the case, I should see at once I dared not allow to myself? I can perceive no use in making up my mind how to act in circumstances in which I am not now and probably will never be. I have enough to occupy me where I find myself, and should certainly be oftener in doubt how to act, if I had bothered my brains how to think in circumstance foreign to me.

"In such thinking, duty is of necessity a comparatively feeble factor, being only duty imagined, not live duty, and the result is the more questionable. The Lord instructed His apostles not to be anxious about what they should say when they were brought before rulers and kings. I will leave the question of duty alone until action is demanded of me. In the meantime, I will do the duty now required of me, which is the only preparation for the duty that is to come."

Although Alexa had not begun to understand Andrew, she had sense and righteousness enough to feel that he was somehow ahead of her, and that it was not likely he and George Crawford would be of one mind in the matter that occupied her, so different were their ways of looking at things—so different indeed the things themselves they thought worth looking at.

She was silent for a moment, then said, "You can at least tell me what you think of gambling."

"I think it is the meanest mode of gaining or losing money a man could find."

"Why do you think so?"

"Because he desires only to gain, and can gain only by his neighbor's loss. One of the two must be the worse for his transaction with the other. Each *must* wish ill to his neighbor!"

"But the risk was agreed upon between them."

"True, but in what hope? Was it not, on the part of each, that he would be the gainer and the other the loser? There is no common cause, nothing but pure opposition of interest."

"Are there not many things in which one must gain and the other lose?"

"There are many things in which one gains and the other loses; but if it is essential to any transaction that only one side shall gain, the thing is not of God."

"What do you think of trading in stocks?"

"I do not know enough about it to have a right to speak."

"You can give your impression."

"I will not give what I do not value."

"Suppose, then, you heard of a man who had made his money so, how would you behave to him?"

"I would not seek his acquaintance."

"If he sought yours?"

"It would be time to ask how he had made his money. Then it would be my business."

"What would make it your business?"

"That he sought my acquaintance. It would then be necessary to know something about him, and the readiest question would be how he had made his money!"

Alexa was silent for some time.

"Do you think God cares about everything?" she said at length.

"Everything," answered Andrew, and she said no more.

Andrew avoided discussion of moral questions, which he regarded as *vermiculate,* and ready to corrupt obedience. "When you have a thing to do," he would say, "you will do it rightly in

105

proportion to your love of right. But do the right, and you will love the right; for by doing it you will see it in a measure as it is, and no one can see the truth as it is without loving it. The more you *talk* about what is right or even about the doing of it, the more you are in danger of exemplifying how loosely theory may be allied to practice. Talk without action saps the very will. Something you have to do is waiting undone all the time, and getting more and more undone. The only refuge is *to do*."

To know the thing he ought to do was a matter of import; to do the thing he knew he ought to do was a matter of life and death to Andrew. He never allowed even a related question to force itself upon him until he had attended to the thing that demanded doing. It was merest common sense!

Alexa had in a manner gotten over her uneasiness at the report of how George was making his money, and their correspondence was not interrupted. But something, perhaps a movement from the world of spirit coming like the wind, had given her one of those motions to betterment which, however occasioned, are the throb of the divine pulse in our lives, the call of the Father, the pull of home, and the guide thither to such as will obey them. She had in consequence again become doubtful about Crawford, and as to whether she was right in corresponding with him. This led to her talk with Andrew, and, while this made her think less of his intellect, it influenced her in a way she neither understood nor even recognized. There are two ways in which one nature may influence another for betterment—the one by strengthening the will, the other by heightening the ideal. Andrew, without even her suspicion of the fact, wrought in the latter way upon Alexa. She grew more uneasy. George was coming home, and how was she to receive him? Nowise bound, they were yet on terms of intimacy; was she to encourage the procession of that intimacy, or to ward off attempts at nearer approach?

Chapter 20.

THE NEW
GEORGE CRAWFORD

George returned, and made an early appearance at Potlurg. Dawtie met him in the court. She did not know him, but involuntarily shrank from him. He frowned. There was a natural repugnance between them; the one was simple, the other double! The one was pure, the other selfish! The one loved her neighbor, the other preyed upon his!

George was a little louder, and his manners were more studied. Alexa felt him overblown and too much at his ease. What little atmosphere there had been about him was gone, and its place was taken by a colored fog. His dress was unobjectionable, and yet attracted notice; perhaps it was too considered. Alexa was disappointed and a little relieved. He looked older, yet more manly—and rather fat. He had more of the confidence women like to see in a man, than was quite pleasant even to the confident Alexa. His speech was not a little infected with the nasality—as easy to catch as hard to get rid of—which I presume the Puritans carried from England to America. On the whole, George was less interesting than Alexa had expected.

He came to her as if he would embrace her, but an instinctive movement on her part sufficed to check him. She threw an additional heartiness into her welcome, and kept him at arm's length. She felt as if she had lost an old friend and not gained a new one. He made himself very agreeable, but that he made himself so, made him less so.

There was more than these changes at work in her; there was

still the underlying doubt concerning him. Although not yet a live soul, she had strong if vague ideas about right and wrong; and although she sought many things a good deal more than righteousness, I do not see what temptation would at once have turned her from its known paths. At the same time I do not see what she had yet, more than hundreds of thousands of other well-meaning women, to secure her from slow decay and final ruin.

They laughed and talked together very like the way they used to, but every *like* is not the same, and they knew there was a difference. George was stung by the sense of it—too much to show that he was vexed. He laid himself out to be the more pleasing, as if determined to make her feel what he was worth—as the man, namely, whom he imagined himself and valued himself on being.

It is an argument for God, to see what fools those make of themselves who, believing there is a God, do not believe *in* Him—children who do not know the Father. Such make up the mass of church and chapelgoers. Let an earthquake or the smallpox break loose among them, and they will show what sort their religion is! George had got rid of the folly of believing in the existence of a God who was either interested in human affairs or careless of them. He naturally found himself more comfortable in consequence; for he never had believed *in* God, and it is awkward *to* believe and *not* believe at the same moment. What he had called his beliefs were as worthy of the name as those of most people; but whether he was better or worse without them hardly interests me, and my philanthropy will scarce serve to make me glad that he was more comfortable.

As they talked, old times came up, and they drew a little nearer, until at last a gentle spring of rose-colored interest began a feeble flow in Alexa's mind. When George took his leave, which he did soon, with the wisdom of one who feared to bore, she went with him to the court, where the gardener was holding his horse. Beside them stood Andrew, talking to the old man, and admiring the beautiful animal in his charge.

"The life of the Creator has run free through every channel up to this creature!" he was saying as they came near.

"What rot!" said George to himself. But to Alexa he said,

"Here's my old friend, the farmer, I declare!" then to Andrew, "How do you do, Mr. Ingram?"

George never forgot a man's name and was regarded, in consequence, for a better fellow than he was. One may remember for reasons that have little to do with good fellowship! He spoke as if they were old friends. "You seem to like the look of the beast!" he said. "*You* ought to know what's what in horses!"

"He is one of the finest horses I ever saw!" answered Andrew. "The man who owns him is fortunate."

"He ought to be a good one!" said George. "I gave a hundred and fifty in guineas for him yesterday!"

Andrew could not help vaguely reflecting what kind of money had bought him, if Sandy was right.

Alexa was pleased to see Andrew. He made her feel more comfortable, and his presence seemed to protect her a little.

"May I ask you, Mr. Ingram," she said, "to repeat what you were saying about the horse as we came up?"

"I was saying," answered Andrew, "that, to anyone who understands a horse, it is clear that the power of God must have flowed unobstructed through many generations to fashion such a perfection."

"Oh! You endorse the development theory, do you?" said George. "I should hardly have expected that of you!"

"I do not think it has anything to do with what I said; no one disputes that this horse comes of many generations of horses! The development theory, if I understand aright, concerns itself with how his first ancestor in his own kind came to be a horse."

"And about that there can be no doubt in the mind of anyone who believes in the Bible!" said George.

"God makes beautiful horses," returned Andrew. "Whether He takes the one way or the other to make them, I am sure He takes the right way."

"You imply it is of little consequence what you believe about it!"

"If I had to make them, it would be of consequence. But what is of consequence is that He makes them, not out of nothing but out of Himself. Why should my poor notion of God's *how* be of importance, so long as when I see a horse like yours, Mr. Crawford, I say, 'God be praised'? It is of eternal importance to love the animal, and see in him the beauty of the Lord; it is of none to fancy that I know which way God took to make him. Not having in me the power or the stuff to make a horse, I cannot know how God made the horse; yet I can know him to be beautiful!"

"But," said George, "the first horse was a very common-looking domestic animal, which they kept to eat—nothing like this one!"

"Then you think God made the first horse, and after that the horses made themselves!" said Andrew.

Alexa laughed, George said nothing, and Andrew went on.

"But," he said, "if we have come up from the lower animals, through a million of kinds, perhaps then I am more than prepared to believe that the man who does not do the part of a man, will have to go down again, through all the stages of his being, to a position beneath the lowest forms of the powers he has misused, and there begin to rise once more, haunted perhaps with dim hints of the world of humanity left so far above him."

"Bah! What's the use of bothering? Rubbish!" cried George, with rude jollity. "You know as well as I do, Mr. Ingram, it's all bosh. Things will go on as they're doing, and as they have been doing till now from all eternity, so far as we know, and that's enough for us!"

"They will not go on for long in our sight, Mr. Crawford! The worms will have a word to say with us!"

Alexa turned away.

"You've not given up preaching and taken to the practical yet, Mr. Ingram, I see!" said George.

Andrew laughed. "I flatter myself I have not ceased to be practical, Mr. Crawford. You are busy with what you see, and I am busy as well with what I don't see; but all the time I believe my farm is in as good a state as your books!"

George gave a start, and stole a look at the young farmer, but was satisfied he meant nothing. The self-seeker will walk into the very abyss protesting himself a practical man, and counting him unpractical who will not with him "jump the life to come." Himself, he neither measures the width nor questions his muscle.

110

Chapter 21.

WHAT IS IT WORTH?

Andrew, with all his hard work—harder since Sandy went—continued able to write, for he neither sought company nor drank strong drink, and he was the sport of no passion. From threatened inroads of temptation, he appealed to Him who created to life His child above the torrent, and made impulse the slave of conscience and manhood. There were no demons riding the whirlwinds of his soul. It is not wonderful then that he should be able to write a book, or that the book should be of genuine and original worth. It had the fortune to be "favorably" reviewed, though scarce one of those who reviewed it understood it, while all of them seemed to themselves to understand it perfectly.

Had the book not been thus received, Alexa would not have bought a copy, or been able to admire it. The review she read was in a paper whose editor would not have admitted it, had he suspected the drift which the reviewer had failed to see; and the passages quoted appealed to Alexa in virtue, partly of her not seeing half of what they involved, or anything whatever of the said drift. But because his book had been published, and because she approved of certain lines, phrases, and passages in it, and chiefly because it had been praised by more than one influential paper, Andrew rose immensely in Alexa's opinion. Although he was the son of a tenant, was even a laborer on his farm, and had covered a birth no higher than that of Jesus Christ with the gown of no university, she began, against her own sense of what was fit, to look up to the plowman. The plowman was not aware of this, and would have been careless had he been. He respected his landlord's daughter, nor ever questioned her superiority as a lady where he made no claim to being a gentleman; but he recognized in her no power either to help or to hurt.

When they next met, Alexa was no longer indifferent to his presence, and even made a movement in the direction of being agreeable to him. She dropped in some measure her patronizing carriage, without knowing she had ever used it, but had the assurance to compliment him not merely on the poem he had written, but on the way it had been received. She could not have credited, had he told her that he was as indifferent to the praise or blame of what is called the public, as if that public were indeed what it is most like—a boy just learning to read. Yet it is the consent of such a public that makes the very essence of what is called fame! How should a man care for it, who knows that he is on his way to join his peers, to be a child with the great ones of the earth, the lovers of the truth, the doers of the Will? What to him is the wind of the world he has left behind, a wind that cannot arouse the dead, that can only blow about the graveclothes of the dead as they bury their dead?

"Live, Dawtie," Andrew had said to the girl, "and one day ye'll have your heart's desire; for 'Blessed are they that hunger and thirst after righteousness!' "

Andrew was neither annoyed nor gratified with the compliments Alexa paid him, for she did not know the informing power of the book—what he cared for in it, the thing that made him write it. But her gentleness and kindness did please him; he was glad to feel a little at home with her, glad to draw a little nearer to one who had never been other than good to him. And then was she not more than kind, even loving, to Dawtie?

"So, Andrew, you are a poet at last!" she said, holding out her hand to him, which Andrew received with a palm that wrote the better verse that it was callused. "Please to remember I was the first to find you out!" she added.

"I think it was my mother!" answered Andrew.

"And I would have helped you if you would have let me!"

"It is not well, ma'am, to push the bird off because he can't sit safe on the edge of the nest!"

112

"Perhaps you are right! A failure then would have stood in the way of your coming fame."

"Oh, for that, ma'am, believe me, I do not care a short straw."

"What do you not care for?"

"For fame."

"That is wrong, Andrew. We ought to care what our neighbors think of us!"

"My neighbors did not set me to do the work, and I did not seek their praise in doing it. Their friendship I prize dearly—more than tongue can tell."

"You cannot surely be so conceited, Andrew, as to think nobody capable of judging your work!"

"Far from it, ma'am! But you were speaking of fame, and that does not come from any wise judgment."

"Then what do you write for, if you care nothing for fame? I thought that was what all poets wrote for!"

"So the world thinks; and those that do, sometimes have their reward."

"Tell me what you write for."

"I write because I want to tell something that makes me glad and strong. I want to say it, and so try to say it. Things come to me in gleams and flashes, sometimes in words themselves, and I want to weave them into a melodious, harmonious whole. I was once at an oratorio, and that taught me the shape of a poem. In a pause of the music, I seemed all at once to see Handel's heavy countenance looking out of his great wig, as he sat putting together his notes, ordering about in his mind, and fixing in their places with his pen, his drums, and pipes, and fiddles, and roaring brass, and flutes, and oboes—all to open the door for the thing that was plaguing him with the confusion of its beauty. For I suppose even Handel did not hear it all clear and plain at first, but had to build his orchestra into a mental organ for his mind to let itself out by, through the many music holes, lest it should burst with its repressed harmonic delights. He must have felt an agonised need to set the haunting angels of sound in obedient order and range, responsive to the soul of the thing, its one ruling idea! I saw him with his white rapt face, looking like a prophet of the living God sent to speak out of the heart of the mystery of truth! I saw him as he sat staring at the

113

paper before him, scratched all over as with the fury of a holy anger at his own impotence, his soul communing with heavenliest harmonies! Ma'am, will any man persuade me that Handel at such a moment was athirst for fame? Or that the desire to please a houseful, or worldful of such as heard his oratorios, gave him the power to write his music? No, ma'am! He was filled, not with the lust of fame, not with the longing for sympathy, and not even with the good desire to give delight, but with the music itself. It was crying in him to get out; and could not rest till he had let it out; and every note that dropped from his pen was a chip struck from the granite wall between the songbirds in their prison nest and the air of their liberty. Creation is God's self-wrought freedom.

"No, ma'am, I do not despise my fellows, but neither do I prize the judgment of more than a few of them. I prize and love the people themselves, but not their opinions."

Alexa was silent, and Andrew took his leave. She sat still for a while thinking. If she did not understand, at least she remembered Andrew's face as he talked. Could presumption make his face shine so? Could presumption make him so forget himself?

Chapter 22.

THE GAMBLER AND
THE COLLECTOR

Things went swimmingly with George. He had weathered a crisis and was now full of confidence, as well as the show of it. That he held himself a man who could do what he pleased, was plain to everyone. His prosperity leaned upon that of certain princes of the power of money in America, and gleaning after them he found his fortune.

But he did not find much increase of favor with Alexa. Her spiritual tastes were growing more refined. There was something about the man which she could no longer contemplate without dissatisfaction. It cost her tears at night to think that, although he had degenerated, he had remained true to her; for she saw plainly that it was only lack of encouragement that prevented him from asking her to be his wife. She knew she must appear changeable, but this was not the man she had been ready to love, for the plant had put forth a flower that was not in sequence with the leaf! The cause of his appearing different might lie in herself, but in any case he was not the gentleman she had thought him! Had she loved him she would have stood by him bravely; but now she could not help recalling the disgrace of the father. Would it be any wonder if the son himself proved less than honorable? She would have broken with him but for one thing—he had become an intimate friend of her father, and the laird enjoyed his company.

George had a straggling acquaintance with many things, and could readily appear to know more than he did. He was, besides, that most agreeable person to a man with a hobby—a good listener—when he saw reason. He made himself so pleasant that the laird was not only always glad to see him, but would often ask him to stay to supper, when he would fish up from the wine cellar he had inherited a bottle with a history and a character, and the two would pass the evening together. Alexa tried not to wish him away, for was not her father happy with him? Though without much pleasure of his own in such things, George, moved by the reflection of the laird's interest, even began to *collect* a little, mainly in the hope of picking up what might gratify the laird; nor, if he came upon a thing he *must* covet, would hesitate to spend on it a good sum. Naturally the old man grew to regard him as a son of the best sort, one who would do anything to please his father, and indulge his tastes.

It may seem surprising that a man such as George should have remained so true; but he had a bulldog tenacity of purpose, as indeed his money-making indicated. There was good in him to the measure of admiring a woman like Alexa, though not of admiring a far better. He saw himself in danger of losing her, and concluded influences at work to the frustration of his own. He surmised that she doubted the character of his business; he feared the clownish farmer-poet might have dazzled with his new reputation her womanly judgment; and he felt himself called upon to make good his position against any and every prejudice she might have conceived against him! He would yield nothing! If he was foiled he was foiled, but it should not be his fault. His own phrase was that he would not throw up the sponge so long as he could come up grinning. He had occasional twinges of discomfort, for his conscience, although seared indeed, was not seared as with the hottest iron, seeing he had never looked straight at any truth. It would ease those twinges, he vaguely imagined, so to satisfy a good woman like Alexa, if she made common cause with him, accepting not merely himself, but the money of which he had at such times a slight loathing. Alexa was handsome—he thought her *very* handsome—and, true to Mammon, he would gladly be true also to something better. There might be another camp, and it would be well to have friends in that too!

So unlike Andrew, how could he but dislike him? And his

dislike was fostered into hatred by his jealousy. Cowed before him, like Macbeth before Banquo, because he was an honest man, how could he but hate him? He thought him a canting sneaking fellow—which he was, if canting consists in giving God His own, and sneaking consists in fearing no man, in fearing nothing, indeed, save doing wrong. How could George consent even to the far-off existence of such a man!

The laird also had taken a dislike to Andrew. From the night when Dawtie made her appeal, he had not known an hour's peace. It was not that it had waked his conscience, though it had made it sleep a little less soundly; it was only that he feared she might take further action in regard to the cup. She seemed to him to be taking part with the owner of the cup against him, for he could not see that she was taking part with himself against the devil—that it was not the cup she was anxious about, but the life of her master. What if she should acquaint the earl's lawyer with all she knew? He would be dragged into public daylight! He could not pretend ignorance concerning the identity of the chalice! That would be to be no antiquarian, while Dawtie would bear witness that he had in his possession a book telling all about it!

But the girl would never of herself have turned against him—it was all that fellow Ingram, with his overstrained and absurd notions as to what God required of His poor sinful creatures! Andrew must not even believe in the atonement! He must not believe that Christ had given satisfaction to the Father for our sins! He demanded in the name of religion more than any properly educated and authorized minister would, and in his meddlesomeness had worried Dawtie into doing as she did! The girl was a good and modest girl, and would never of herself have so acted; while Andrew was righteous overmuch, therefore eaten up with self-conceit and with the notion of pleasing God more than other men. Yes, he cherished old grudges against him, and would be delighted to bring his old schoolmaster to shame! He was not a bad boy when at school, and the laird had always liked him; the change in him witnessed to the peril of extremes. Here they had led to spiritual pride, which was the worst of all the sins! The favorite of heaven could have no respect for the opinion of his betters, and Andrew the man was bent on returning evil for all the good done to Andrew the boy! It was a happy thing young Crawford understood him—*he* would be his friend, and defeat the machination of his enemy! If only the fellow's lease were out,[18] he would get rid of him.

Moved by George's sympathy with his tastes, the laird drew nearer and nearer to disclosing the possession which was the pride of his life. The enjoyment of connoisseur or collector rests much on the glory of possession—of having what another has not or, better still, what no other can possibly have.

From what he had long ago seen on the night of the storm, and now from the way the old man hinted and talked and broke off, also from the uneasiness he sometimes manifested, George had guessed that there was something over whose possession he gloated, but for whose presence among his treasures he could not comfortably account. He therefore set himself, without asking a single question, to make the laird unbosom his secret. A hold on the father would make a hold on the daughter!

One day in a pawnbroker's shop, George lighted upon a rarity indeed. It might or might not have the history attributed to it, but was in itself more than interesting for the beauty of both material and workmanship. The sum asked for it was large, but with the chance of pleasing the laird, it seemed to George but a trifle. It was also, he judged, of intrinsic value to a great part of the price. Had he been then aware of the special passion of the old man for jewels, he would have been yet more eager to secure it for him. It was a watch, not very small, and by no means thin—a repeater, whose bell was dulled by the stones of the mine in which it lay buried. The case was one mass of gems of considerable size, and of every color. Ruby, sapphire, and emerald were judiciously parted by diamonds of utmost purity, while yellow diamonds took the golden place for which the topaz had not been counted of sufficient value. They were all crusted together as close as they could lie, their setting hardly showing. The face was of fine opals, across which moved the two larger hands radiant with rubies, while the second hand flitted flashing around, covered with tiny diamonds. The numerals were in sapphires, within a bordering ring of emeralds and black pearls. The jewel was a splendor of color and light.

When he returned to Potlurg, George took it from his

pocket, held it a moment in the sunlight, and handed it to the laird. The older man glowered at it, and saw an angel from heaven in a thing compact of earth-chips! As near as anything can be loved of a live soul, the laird loved a fine stone; what in it he loved most—the color, the light, the shape, the value, or the mystery—he could not have told! And here was a jewel of many fine stones! With both hands he pressed it to his bosom. He looked at it in the sun, then went into the shadow and looked at it again. Suddenly he thrust it into his pocket and hurried, followed by George, to his study. There he closed the shutters, lighted a lamp, and gazed at the marvel, turning it in all directions. At length he laid it on the table, and sank with a sigh into a chair.

George understood the sigh, and dug its source deeper by telling him, as he had heard it, the story of the jewel. "It may be true," George ended. "I remember seeing some time ago a description of the toy. I think I could lay my hand on it!"

"Would you mind leaving it with me till you come again?" faltered the laird.

He knew he could not buy it—he had not the money, but he would gladly dally with the notion of being its possessor. To part with it, the moment after having held it in his hand and gloated over it for the first time, would be too keen a pain! It was unreasonable to have to part with it at all! He *ought* to be its owner! Who could be such an owner to a thing like that as he? It was a wrong to him that it was not his! Next to his cup, it was the most precious thing he had ever wished to possess. A thing for a man to take to the grave with him! Was there *no* way of carrying *any* treasure to the other world? He would have sold of his land to secure the miracle, but, alas, it was all entailed! For a moment the Cellini chalice seemed of less account, and he felt ready to throw open the window of his treasure room and pitch everything out. The demon of *having* is as imperious and as capricious as that of drink, and there is no refuge from it but with the Father. "This kind goeth not out but by prayer."

The poor slave uttered not a sigh now, but a groan. "You'll tell the man," he said, thinking George had borrowed the thing to show him, "that I did not even ask the price. I know I cannot buy it."

"Perhaps he would give you credit," suggested George with a

smile.

"No! I will have nothing to do with credit! I should not be able to call it my own." Money honesty, at least, was still strong in the laird. "But," he continued, "do try and persuade him to let me have it for a day or two—that I may learn its beauty by heart, and think of it all the days and dream of it all the nights of my life after!"

"There will be no difficulty about that," answered George. "The owner will be delighted to let you keep it as long as you wish!"

"I would it were so."

"It *is* so."

"You don't mean to say, George, that that queen of jewels is yours, and you will lend it to me?"

"The thing is mine, but I will not lend it—not even to you, sir!"

"I don't wonder! I don't wonder! But it is a great disappointment. I was beginning to hope I—I might have the loan of it for a week or two even!"

"You should indeed if the thing were mine!" said George, playing him. "But—"

"Oh, I beg your pardon! I thought you said it was yours."

"So it was when I bought it, but it is mine no longer. It is yours. I purchased it for you this morning."

The old man was speechless. He rose, and seizing George by both hands, stood staring at him. Something very like tears gathered within the reddened rims of his eyes. He had grown pale and feebler of late, ever in vain devising secure possession of the cup—possession moral as well as legal. But this entrancing gift brought with it strength and hope in regard to the chalice! "To him that hath shall be given!" quoted the Mammon within him.

"George!" he said, with a moan of ecstasy, "you are my good angel!" and sat down exhausted.

The watch was George's key to the laird's "closet," as he persisted in calling his treasury. In old times not a few houses in Scotland held a certain tiny room, built for the head of the family, to be his closet for prayer. It was, I believe, with the notion of such a room in his head, that the laird had called his museum his closet. And he was more right than he meant to be,

120

for in that chamber he did his truest worship—truest as to the love in it, falsest as to its object; for there he worshiped the god vilest bred of all the gods, bred namely of man's distrust in the Life of the Universe.

And now here also were two met together to worship; for from this time the laird, disclosing his secret, made George free in his sanctuary.

George was by this time able to take a genuine interest in the collection. But he was much amused, sometimes annoyed, with the behavior of the laird in his closet—he was more nervous and touchy over his things than a she-bear over her cubs.

Of all dangers to his darlings he thought a woman the worst, and had therefore seized with avidity the chance of making that room a hidden one, the possibility of which he had spied almost the first moment he entered it.

He became, if possible, fonder of his things than ever, and flattered himself he had found in George a fellow worshiper. George's exaggerated or pretended appreciation only enhanced his sense of their value.

Chapter 23.

ON THE MOOR

Alexa had a strong shaggy pony, which she rode the oftener that George came so often, taking care to be well gone before he arrived on his beautiful horse.

One lovely summer evening she had been across the moor a long way, and was returning as the sun went down. A glory of molten red gold was shining in her face, so that she could see nothing in front of her, and so was startled by a voice greeting her with a respectful good evening. The same moment she was alongside the speaker in the blinding veil of the sun. It was Andrew walking home from a village on the other side of the moor. She drew rein, and they went together.

"What has come to you, Mr. Ingram!" she said. "I hear you were at church last Sunday evening!"

"Why should I not be, ma'am?" asked Andrew.

"For the reason that you are not in the way of going."

"There might be good reason for going once, or for going many times, and yet not for going always."

"We won't begin with quarreling! There are things we shall not agree about!"

"Yes, one or two—for a time, I believe!" returned Andrew.

"What did you think of Mr. Rackstraw's sermon? I suppose you went to hear *him!*"

"Yes, ma'am—at least partly."

"Well?"

"Will you tell me first whether you were satisfied with Mr.

Rackstraw's teaching? I know you were there."

"I was quite satisfied."

"Then I don't see reason for saying anything about it."

"If I am wrong, you ought to try to set me right!"

"The Prophet Elisha would have done no good by throwing his salt into the running stream. He cast it, you will remember, into the spring."

"I do not understand you."

"There is no use in persuading a person to change an opinion."

"Why not?"

"Because the man is neither the better nor the worse for it. If you had told me you were distressed to hear a man in authority speak as Mr. Rackstraw spoke concerning a being you loved, I would have tried to comfort you by pointing out how false it was. But if you are content to hear God so represented, why should I seek to convince you of what is valueless to you? Why offer you to drink what your heart is not thirsting after? Would you love God more because you found He was not what you were quite satisfied He should be?"

"Do tell me more plainly what you mean!"

"You must excuse me. I have said all I will. I cannot reason in defense of God. It seems blasphemy to argue that His nature is not such as no honorable man could love in another person."

"But if the Bible says so?"

"If the Bible said so, the Bible would be false. But the Bible does not say so."

"How is it then that it seems to say so?"

"Because you were taught falsely about Him before you desired to know Him."

"But I am capable of judging now!"

Andrew was silent.

"Am I not?" insisted Alexa.

"Do you desire to know God?" said Andrew.

"I think I do know Him."

"And you think those things true?"

"Yes."

"Then we are where we were, and I say no more."

"You are not polite."

"I cannot help it. I must let you alone to believe about God what you can. You will not be blamed for not believing what you cannot."

"Do you mean that God never punishes anyone for what he cannot help?"

"Assuredly."

"How do you prove that?"

"I will not attempt to prove it. If you are content to think He does, if it does not trouble you that your God should be unjust, go on thinking so until you are made miserable by it; then I will pour out my heart to deliver you."

She was struck, not with any truthfulness in what he said, but with the evident truthfulness of the man himself. Right or wrong, there was about him a certain radiance of conviction, which certainly was not around Mr. Rackstraw.

"The things that can be shaken," said Andrew, as if thinking with himself, "may last for a time; but they will at length be shaken to pieces, that the things which cannot be shaken may show what they are. Whatever we call religion will vanish when we see God face to face."

For a while they went brushing through the heather in silence.

"May I ask you one question, Mr. Ingram?" said Alexa.

"Surely, ma'am. Ask anything you like."

"And you will answer me?"

"If I am at liberty to answer you, I will."

"What do you mean by being at liberty? Are you under any vow?"

"I am under the law of love! I am bound to do nothing to hurt. An answer that would do you no good, I will not give."

"How do you know what will or will not do me good?"

"I must use what judgment I have."

"Is it true, then, that you believe God gives you whatever you ask?"

"I have never asked anything of Him that He did not give me."

"Would you mind telling me anything you have asked of Him?"

"I have never yet asked anything not included in the prayer, 'Thy will be done!' "

"That will be done without your praying for it!"

"Pardon me! I do not believe it will be done, to all eternity, without my praying for it. Where first am I accountable that His will should be done? Is it not in myself? How is His will to be done in me without my willing it? Does He not want me to love what He loves? To be like Himself? To do His will with the glad effort of my will? In a word, to will what He wills? And when I find I cannot, what am I to do but pray for help? I pray, and He helps me."

"There is nothing strange in that!"

"Surely not! It seems to me the simplest common sense. It is my business, and the business of every man, that God's will be done by our obedience to that will, the moment we know it."

"I fancy you are not so different from other people as you think yourself! But they say you want to die."

"I want nothing but what God wants. I desire righteousness."

"Then you accept the righteousness of Christ?"

"Accept it! I long for it!"

"You know that is not what I mean."

"I seek first the kingdom of God and God's righteousness."

"You avoid my question! Do you accept the righteousness of Christ instead of your own?"

"I have no righteousness of my own to put it instead of. The only righteousness there is, is God's, and He will make me righteous like Himself. He is not content that only His Son should be righteous as He is righteous. The thing is plain; I will not argue about it."

"You do not believe in the atonement!"

"I believe in Jesus Christ. He is the atonement. What strength God has given me, I will spend in knowing Him and doing what He tells me. To interpret His plans before we know Him is to mistake both Him and His plans. I know this, that He has given His life for what multitudes, who call themselves by His name, would not rise from their seats to share in!"

"You think me incapable of understanding the Gospel?"

"I think if you did understand the Gospel of Christ, you would be incapable of believing the things about His Father that you say you do believe. But I will not say a word more. When you are able to see the truth, you will see it; and when you desire the truth you will be able."

Alexa touched her pony with her whip. But by and by she

pulled him up, and made him walk until Andrew overtook her. The sun was by this time far out of sight, the glow of the west was over, and twilight lay upon the world. It's ethereal dimness had sunk into her soul.

"Does the gloaming[19] make you sad, Mr. Ingram?" she asked.

"It makes me very quiet," he answered, "as if all my people were asleep, and waiting for me."

"Do you mean as if they were all dead? How can you talk of it so quietly?"

"Because I do not believe in death."

"What *do* you mean?"

"I am a Christian!"

"I hope you are, Mr. Ingram, though to be honest with you, some things make me doubt it. Perhaps you would say I am not a Christian."

"It is enough that God knows whether you are a Christian or not. Why should I say you are or are not?"

"But I want to know what you meant when you said you were a Christian. How should that make you indifferent to the death of your friends? Death is a dreadful thing, look at it how you like!"

"The Lord says, 'He that liveth and believeth in Me shall never die.' If my friends are not dead, but living and waiting for me, why should I wait for them in a fierce, stormy night, or a black frost, instead of the calm of such a sleeping day as this—a day with the sun hid, as Shakespeare calls it!"

"How you do mix up things! Shakespeare and Jesus Christ!"

"God mixed them first, and will mix them a good deal more yet!" said Andrew.

But for the smile which would hover about his mouth, his way of answering would sometimes have seemed curt to those who did not understand him. Instead of holding aloof in his superiority, however, as some thought he did when he would not answer, or answered abruptly, Andrew's soul would be hovering, watching and hoping for a chance of lighting, and giving of the best he had. He was like a great bird changing parts with a child—the child afraid of the bird, and the bird enticing the child to be friends. He had learned that if he poured out his treasure recklessly, it might be received with dishonor, and but choke the way of the chariot of approaching Truth.

"Perhaps you will say next there is no such thing as suffering!" resumed Alexa.

"No; the Lord said that in the world His friends should have tribulation."

"What tribulation have you, who are so specially His friend?"

"Not much yet. It is a little, however, sometimes, to know such strong, and beautiful, and happy-making things, and all the time my people, my beloved humans, born of my Father in heaven, with the same heart for joy and sorrow, will not listen and be comforted. I think that was what made our Lord sorriest of all."

"Mr. Ingram, I have no patience with you! How dare you liken your trouble to that of our Lord—making yourself equal with Him!"

"Is it making myself equal with Him to say that I understand a little how He felt toward His fellowmen? I am always trying to understand Him; would it be a wonder if I did sometimes a little? How is a man to do as He did without understanding Him?"

"Are you going to work miracles next?"

"Jesus was always doing what God wanted Him to do. That was what He came for, not to work miracles. He could have worked a great many more if He had pleased, but He did no more than God wanted of Him. Am I not to try to do the will of God, just because He who died that I might not, always succeeded, however hard it was, while I am always falling and having to try again?"

"And you think you will come to it in this life?"

"I never think about that; I only think about doing His will *now*, not about doing it *then*—that is, tomorrow or the next day or the next world. I know only one life—the life that is hid with Christ in God; and that is the life by which I live here and now. I do not make schemes of life; I live. Life will teach me God's plans; I will take no trouble about them; I will only obey and receive the bliss He sends me. And of all things, I will not make theories of God's plans for other people to accept. I will only do my best to destroy such theories as I find coming between some poor glooming heart and the sun shining in his strength. Those who love the shade of lies, let them walk in it until the shiver of the eternal cold drives them to seek the face of Jesus Christ. To appeal to their intellect would be but to drive them the deeper into the shade to justify their being in it. And if by argument you did persuade them out of it, they would but run into a deeper and worse darkness."

"How could that be?"

"They would at once think that by an intellectual stride they had advanced in the spiritual life, whereas they would be neither the better nor the worse. I know a man, once among the foremost in denouncing the old theology, who is now no better than a swindler. His intellectual freedom seems only to have served his spiritual subjugation. Right opinion, except it spring from obedience to the truth, is but so much rubbish on the golden floor of the temple."

The peace of the night and its luminous earnestness were gleaming on Andrew's face; and Alexa, glancing up as he ceased, felt again the inroad of a sense of something in the man that was not in the other men she knew—the spiritual shadow of a dweller in regions beyond her understanding. The man was before her, yet out of her sight!

The whole thing was too simple for her, for only a child could understand it. Instead of listening to the elders and priests to learn how to save his soul, Andrew cast away all care of himself, left that to God, and gave himself to do the will of Him from whose heart he came, even as the Eternal Life, the Son of God, required of him; in the mighty hope of becoming one mind, heart, soul, one eternal being, with Him, with the Father, and with every good man, and walking in the world as Enoch[20] walked with God, held by His hand. This is what man was and is meant to be, what man must become; thither the wheels of time are roaring; thither work all the silent potencies of the eternal world; and they that will not awake and arise from the dead, must be flung from their graves by the throes of a shivering world.

When he had done speaking, Andrew stood, looking up. A few stars were looking down through the limpid air. Alexa rode on. Andrew let her go and walked after her alone, sure that her mind must one day open to the eternal fact that God is all in all, the perfect Friend of His children; yea, that He would sooner cease to be God than fail His child in his battle with Death.

Chapter 24.

THE WOOER

Alexa kept hoping that George would be satisfied she was not inclined toward him as she had been; and that, instead of bringing the matter to open issue, he would continue to come and go as the friend of her father. But George came to the conclusion that he ought to remain in doubt no longer, and one afternoon followed her into the garden. She had gone there with a certain half-scientific, half-religious book in her hand, from which she was storing her mind with arguments against what she supposed the opinions of Andrew. She had, however, little hope of his condescending to front them with counterargument. His voice returned ever to the ear of her mind in words like these, "If you are content to think so, you are in no condition to receive what I have to communicate. Why should I press water on a soul that is not thirsty? Let us wait for the drought of the desert, when life is a low fever, and the heart is dry; when the earth is like iron, and the heavens above it are as brass!"

She started at the sound of George's voice.

"What lovely weather!" he said.

Even lovers betake themselves to the weather as a medium—the side of Nature which all understand. It was a good old-fashioned, hot summer afternoon, one ill-chosen for the pursuit of love.

"Yes?" answered Alexa, with a subaudible point of interrogation, and held her book so that he might feel it on the point of being lifted again to eager eyes. But he was more sentimental than sensitive.

"Please put your book down for a moment. I have not of late asked too much of your attention, Alexa!"

"You have been very kind, George!" she answered.

"Kind in not asking much of your attention?"

"Yes—that, and giving my father so much of yours."

"I certainly have seen more of him than of you!" returned George, hoping her words meant reproach. "But he has always been kind to me, and pleased to see me! You have not given me too much encouragement."

To begin wooing with complaint is not wise, and George felt that he had fallen into the wrong track; and Alexa took care that he should not get out of it easily. Not being simple, he always settled the best course to pursue, and often went wrong. The man who cares only for what is true and right is saved much thinking and planning. He generally sees but one way of doing a thing!

"I am glad to hear you say so, George! You have not mistaken me."

"You were not so sharp with me when I went away, Alexa!"

"No. Then you were going away."

"Should you not show a fellow some kindness when he has come back?"

"Not when he does not seem content with having come back."

"I do not understand."

But Alexa gave no explanation.

"You would be kind to me again if I were going away again?"

"Perhaps."

"That is, if you were sure I was not coming back?"

"I did not *say* so."

"I can't make it out, Alexa! I used to think there could never be any misunderstanding between you and me. But something has crept in between us, and for the life of me I do not know what it is."

"There is one thing for which I am more obliged to you than I can tell—that you did not say anything before you went."

"I am awfully sorry for it now, but I thought you understood."

"I did, and I am very glad, for I should have repented it long ago."

This was hardly logical, but George seemed to understand.

"You are cruel!" he said. "I should have made it the business of my life that you never did!" Yet George knew of things he dared not tell, that had taken place almost as soon as he was relieved from the sustaining and restraining human pressure in which he had grown up.

"I am certain I should," persisted Alexa.

"Why are you so certain?"

"Because I am so glad now to think I am free."

"Someone has been maligning me, Alexa! It is very hard not to know where the stab comes from!"

"The testimony against you is from your own lips, George. I heard you talking to my father, and was aware of a tone I did not like. I listened more attentively, and became convinced that your ways of thinking had deteriorated. There seemed not a remnant left of the honor I thought characterized you!"

"Why, certainly, as an honest man, I cannot talk religion like your friend the farmer!"

"Do you mean that Andrew Ingram is not an honest man?" rejoined Alexa, with some heat.

"I mean that I am an honest man."

"I am doubtful of you."

"I can tell the quarter whence that doubt was blown!"

"It would be of greater consequence to blow it away! George Crawford, do you believe yourself an honest man?"

"As men go, yes!"

"But not as men go, George? As you would like to appear to the world when hearts are as open as faces?"

He was silent.

"Would the way you have made your money stand the scrutiny of—?" She had Andrew in her mind, and was on the point of saying "Jesus Christ," but felt she had no right, and hesitated.

"—of our friend Andrew?" supplemented George, with a spiteful laugh. "The only honest mode of making money he knows is the strain of his muscles—the farmer way! He wouldn't keep back his corn for a better market, not he!"

"It so happens that I know he would not. He and my father had a dispute on that very point, and I heard them. Andrew said poor people were not to go hungry that he might get rich.

He was not sent into the world to make money, he said, but to grow corn. The corn was grown, and he could get enough for it now to live by, and had no right and no desire to get more, and he would not keep it back! The land was God's, not his, and the poor were God's children, and had their rights from Him! He was sent to grow corn for them!"

"And what did your father say to that wisdom?"

"That is no matter. Nor do I profess to understand Mr. Ingram. I only know," added Alexa, with a little laugh, "that he is consistent, for he has puzzled me all my life. I can, however, see a certain nobility in him that sets him apart from other men!"

"And I can see that when I left I was needlessly modest! I thought *my* position too humble!"

"What am I to understand by that?"

"What you think I mean."

"I wish you a good afternoon, Mr. Crawford!"

Alexa rose and left him.

George had indeed grown coarser. He turned where he stood with his hands in his pockets, and looked after her; then he smiled to himself a nasty smile, and said, "At least I have made her angry, and that's something! What has a fellow like that to give her? Poet, indeed! What's that? He's not even the rustic gentleman! He's downright vulgar—a clodhopper born and bred! But the lease, I understand, will soon be out, and Potlurg will never let him renew it! *I* will see to that! The laird hates the canting scoundrel. I would rather pay Fordyce double the rent myself!"

His behavior after that day did not put Andrew's manners in the shade! Though he never said a word to flatter Alexa, he spoke often in a way she did not at all like, persistently refused to enter into argument with her where most she desired it, and yet his every tone, every movement toward her was full of respect. And however she strove against the idea, she felt him her superior, and had indeed begun to wish that she had never shown herself at a disadvantage by the assumption of superiority. It would be pleasant to know that it pained him to disapprove of her! For she began to feel that as she disapproved of George, and could not like him, so the young farmer disapproved of her and could not like her. It was a new and by no means agreeable thought. Andrew delighted in beautiful things, and he did not see anything beautiful in her! Alexa was not conceited, but she knew she was handsome, and also knew that Andrew would never feel one heartthrob more because of any beauty such as hers. Had he not as good as told her she was of the dead who would not come alive! It would be something to be loved by a man like that! But Alexa was too maidenly to think of any man pursuing her; and even if he loved her, she could not marry a man in Andrew's position. She might stretch a point or two were the lack but a point or two; but there was no stretching points to the marrying of a peasant without education, who worked on his father's farm. The thing was ridiculous, and the very idea too absurd to pass through her idlest thought! But she was not going to marry George—that was well settled. In a year or two he would be quite fat! And he always had his hands in his pockets! There was something about him *not* like a gentleman. He suggested an auctioneer, or a cheapjack.[21]

But George had no intention of forsaking the house—not yet, at least. He was bent on humbling his cousin, therefore continued his relations with her father, while he hurried on, as fast as consistent with good masonry, the building of a house on a small estate that he had bought in the neighborhood, intending it to be an enticement to any lady. So long had he regarded everything through the veil of money that he could not think even of Alexa without thinking of Mammon as well. By this time also he was so much infected with the old man's passion for things curious and valuable, that the idea of one day calling the laird's wonderful collection his own had a real part in his desire to become the daughter's husband. He would not accept her dismissal as final!

Chapter 25.

THE HEART OF THE HEART

The laird had been poorly for some weeks, and Alexa began to fear that he was failing. Nothing more had passed between him and Dawtie, but he knew that anxious eyes were often watching him, and the thought worried him not a little. If he would but take a start, thought Dawtie, and not lose all the good of this life! It was too late for him to rise very high; he could not now be a saint, but he might at least set a foot on the eternal stair that leads to the fullness of bliss! He would have a sore fight with all those imps of *things* before he ceased to love that which was not lovely, and to covet that which was not good! But the man gained a precious benefit from this world, who but began to repent before he left it. If only the laird would start up the hill before his body got quite to the bottom! Was there any way to approach him again with her petition that he would be good to himself, good to God, good to the universe, that he would love what was worth loving, and cast away what was not? She had no light and could do nothing.

Suddenly the old man failed, quite apparently from no cause but weakness. The unease of his mind, the haunting of the dread thought of having to part with the chalice, had induced it. He was in his closet one night late into the morning, and the next day did not get up to breakfast. He said he wanted a little rest. In a day he would be well. But the hour to rise never again came. He seemed very troubled at times, and very desirous of getting up, but was never able. It became necessary to sit with him at night. In fits of delirium he would make a fierce endeavor to rise, insisting that he must go to his study. His closet he never mentioned; even in dreams was his secrecy dominant.

Dawtie, who had her share in nursing him, kept hoping her opportunity would come. He did not seem to cherish any resentment against her. His illness would protect him, he thought, from further intrusion of her conscience upon his, for she must know better than irritate a sick man with over-officiousness! Everybody could not be a saint! It was enough to be a Christian like other good and salvable Christians. It was enough for him if through the merits of his Saviour he gained admission to the heavenly kingdom at last! He never thought how, once in, he could bear to stay in; never thought how heaven could be to him other than the dullest place in the universe of God, more wearisome than the kingdom of darkness itself! And all the time the young woman with the savior-heart was watching by his bedside, ready to speak; but the Spirit gave her no utterance, and her silence soothed his fear of her.

One night he was more restless than usual. Waking from his troubled slumber, he called her, in the tone of one who had something important to communicate.

"Dawtie," he said, with a feeble voice, but glittering eye, "there is no one I can trust like you. I have been thinking ever since of what you said that night. Go to my closet and bring me the cup."

Dawtie held a moment's debate whether it would be right; but she reflected that it made little difference whether the object of his passion was in his hand or in his closet, while it was all the same deep in his heart. His words seemed to imply that he wanted to take his farewell of it; to refuse his request might only fan the evil love, and turn him from the good motion in his mind. She said, "Yes, sir," and stood waiting. He did not speak.

"I do not know where to find it," she said.

"I am going to tell you," he replied, but seemed to hesitate.

"I will not touch a single thing beside," said Dawtie.

He believed her, and at once proceeded. "Take my bunch of keys from the hook behind me. There is the key of the closet door! And there, the key of all the bunch that looks the commonest, but is in reality the most cunningly devised, is the key of the cabinet in which I keep it!"

Then he told her where, behind a little bookcase which moved from the wall on hinges, she would find the cabinet, and in what part of it the cup, wrapped in a piece of silk that had once been a sleeve worn by Madame de Genlis,[22] which did not make Dawtie much wiser.

She went, found the chalice, and brought it where the laird lay waiting for it as a man at the point of death might await the sacramental cup from the absolving priest.

His hands trembled as he took it, for they were the hands of a lover—strange as that love was, which not merely looked for no return, but desired to give neither pleasure nor good to the thing loved! It was no love of the merely dead, but a love of the unliving! He pressed the thing to his bosom; then, as if rebuked by the presence of Dawtie, put it a little from him, and began to pore over every stone, every relieved figure between, and every engraved ornament around the gems, each of which he knew by shape, order, quality of color, better than ever the face of wife or child. But soon his hands sank on the counterpane of silk patchwork, and he lay still, grasping tight the precious thing.

He woke with a start and a cry, to find it safe in both his hands.

"Ugh!" he said. "I thought someone had me by the throat! You didn't try to take the cup from me, did you, Dawtie?"

"No, sir," answered Dawtie. "I would not care to take it out of your hand, but I should be glad to take it out of your heart!"

"If they would only bury it with me!" he murmured, heedless of her words.

"O sir! Would you have it burning your heart to all eternity? Give it up, sir, and take the treasure that thief never stole."

"Yes, Dawtie, yes! That is true treasure!"

"And to get it we must sell all that we have!"

"He gives and withholds as *He* sees fit."

"Then, when you go down into the blackness, longing for the cup you will never see more, you will complain of God that He would not give you your strength to fling it from you?"

He hugged the chalice. "Fling it from me?" he cried fiercely. "Girl, who are you to torment me before my time!"

"Tell me, sir," persisted Dawtie, "why did the apostle cry, 'Awake thou that sleepest!' if they couldn't move?"

"No one can move without God."

"Therefore, seeing everyone can move, it must be God giving them the power to do what He requires of them; we are fearfully to blame for not using the strength God gives us!"

"I cannot bear the strain of thinking!" gasped the laird.

"Then give up thinking, and *do* the thing! Shall I take it for you?"

She put out her hand as she spoke.

"No! No!" he cried, grasping the cup tighter. "You shall not touch it. You would give it to the earl! I know you! Saints hate what is beautiful!"

"I like better to look at things in my Father's hand than in my own!"

"You want to see my cup—it *is* my cup—in the hands of that spendthrift fool, Lord Borland!"

"It is in the Father's hand, whoever has it."

"Hold your tongue, Dawtie, or I will cry out and wake the house!"

"They will think you out of your mind, and come and take the cup from you. Do let me put it away; then you will go to sleep."

"I will not. I cannot trust you with it! You have destroyed my confidence in you! I *may* fall asleep, but if your hand comes within a foot of the cup, it will wake me! I know it will! I shall sleep with my heart on the cup, and the least touch will wake me!"

"I wish you would let Andrew Ingram come and see you, sir!"

"What's the matter with him?"

"Nothing's the matter with him, sir; but he helps everybody to do what is right."

"Conceited rascal! Do you take me for a maniac that you talk such foolery?"

His look was so wild and his faded blue eyes gleamed with such a light of mingled fear and determination that Dawtie was almost sorry she had spoken. With trembling hands he drew the cup within the bedclothes and lay still. If the morning would but come, and bring George Crawford! *He* would restore the cup to its place, or hide it where the laird should know it safe and not far from him!

Dawtie sat motionless, and the old man fell into another feverish doze. She dared not stir lest he should start awake to defend his idol. She sat like an image, moving only her eyes.

"What are you about, Dawtie?" he said at length. "You are after some mischief, you are so quiet!"

"I was telling God how good you would be if He could get you to give up your odds and ends, and take Him instead."

"How dared you say such a thing, sitting there by my side! Are *you* to say to Him that any sinner would be good, if He would only do so and so with him? Tremble, girl, at the vengeance of the Almighty!"

"We are told to make prayers and intercessions for all men, and I was saying what I could for you." The laird was silent, and the rest of the night passed quietly.

His first words in the morning were, "Go and tell your mistress I want her."

When his daughter came, he told her to send for George Crawford. He was worse and wanted to see him.

Alexa thought it best to send Dawtie with the message by the next train. Dawtie did not relish the mission, for she had no faith in Crawford, and did not like his influence on her master. Nonetheless, when she reached his hotel, she insisted on seeing him, and giving her message in person; which done, she made haste for the first train back; they could not do well without her!

But when she arrived at her station, there was Mr. Crawford already on the platform! She endured his company on the journey, but when they reached their destination, she set out for Potlurg on foot as fast as she could. But she had not gone farther than halfway when he overtook her in a hired fly, and insisted she should get in.

Chapter 26.

GEORGE AND DAWTIE

"What is the matter with your master?" George asked Dawtie as they bounced along toward Potlurg.

"God knows, sir."

"What is the use of telling me that? I want you to tell me what *you* know."

"I don't know anything, sir."

"What do you think, then?"

"I should think old age had something to do with it, sir."

"Likely enough, but you know more than that!"

"I shouldn't wonder, sir, if he were troubled in his mind."

"What makes you think so?"

"It is reasonable to think so, sir. He knows he must die before long, and it is dreadful to leave everything you care for, and go where there is nothing you care for!"

"How do you know there is nothing he would care for?"

"What is there, sir, he would be likely to care for?"

"There is his wife! He was fond of her, I suppose, and you pious people fancy you will see each other again!"

"The thought of seeing her would give him little comfort, I am afraid, in parting with the things he has here. He does believe a little, somehow, but I can't understand how."

"What does he believe?"

"He believes a little—he is not sure—that what a man soweth he shall also reap."

"How do you know what he is or is not sure of? It can't be a

139

matter of interest to you."

"Those that come of one Father must have interest in one another."

"How am I to tell we come of one Father, as you call Him? I like to have a thing proved before I believe it. I know neither where I came from nor where I am going; how then can I know that we come from the same Father?"

"I don't know how you're to know it, sir. I take it for granted, and find it good. But there is one thing I am sure of."

"What is that?"

"That if you were my master's friend, you would not rest till you got him to do what was right before he died!"

"I will not be father-confessor to any man! I have enough to do with myself. A good worthy old man like the laird must know better than any other what he ought to do."

"There is no doubt of that, sir."

"What do you want then?"

"To get him to do it. That he knows is what makes it so miserable. If he did not know, he would not be to blame. He knows what it is and won't do it, and that makes him wretched—as it ought, thank God!"

"You're a nice Christian! Thanking God for making a man miserable! Well!" George thought a little. "What would you have me persuade him to?" he asked, for he might hear something it would be useful to know.

But Dawtie had no right and no inclination to tell him what she knew. "I only wish you would persuade him to do what he knows he ought to do," she replied.

Chapter 27.

THE WATCH

George stayed with the laird a good while, and held a long broken talk with him. When he went, Alexa came, thinking her father seemed happier. George had put the cup away for him. Alexa sat with him that night, knowing nothing of the precious thing that was in the house with them.

In the middle of the night, as Alexa was arranging his pillows, the laird drew from under the bedclothes, and held up to her the jeweled watch, flashing in the light of the one candle. She stared. The old man was pleased at her surprise and evident admiration. She held out her hand for it. He gave it to her.

"That watch," he said, "is believed to have belonged to Ninon de Lenclos.[23] It *may*, but I doubt to myself. It is well known she never took presents from her admirers, and she was too poor to have bought such a thing. Madame de Maintenon,[24] however, or some one of her lady friends, might have given it her! It will be yours one day—that is, if you marry the man I should like you to marry."

"Dear father, do not talk of marrying! I have enough with you!" cried Alexa, and felt as if she hated George.

"Unfortunately, you cannot have me always!" returned her father. "I will say nothing more now, but I desire you to consider what I have said."

Alexa put the watch in his hand.

"I trust you do not suppose," she said, "that a houseful of things like that would make any difference."

He looked up at her sharply. A houseful! What did she know? It silenced him, and he lay thinking. Surely the delight of lovely things must be in every woman's heart! Was not the passion, developed or undeveloped, universal? Could a child of his not care for such things?

"Ah," he said to himself, "she takes after her mother."

A wall seemed to rise between him and his daughter. Alas! Alas! The things he loved, and must one day yield, would not be cherished by her. No tender regard would hover around them when he was gone. She would be no protecting divinity to them. God in heaven, she might—she would—he was sure she would sell them!

The sole possible comfort of avarice, as it passes empty and hungry into the empty regions, is that the things it can no more see with eyes or handle with hands will yet be *together* somewhere. Hence the rich leave to the rich, avoiding the man who most needs, or would best use their money. I wonder, is there a lurking notion in the man of much goods that in the still watches of the night, when others sleep, he will return to look on what he leaves behind him? Does he forget the torture of seeing it at the command and in the enjoyment of another—his will concerning this thing or that now but a mockery? Does he know that he who presently holds them will not be able to conceive of their having been another's, as now they are his?

As Alexa sat in the dim light by her brooding father, she loathed the shining thing he had again drawn under the bedclothes, shrank from it as from a manacle the devil had tried to slip on her wrist. The judicial assumption of society suddenly appeared in the emptiness of its arrogance. Marriage for the sake of *things!* Was she not a live soul, made for better than that? She was ashamed of the innocent momentary pleasure the glittering toy had given her.

The laird now and then cast a glance at her face and sighed. He gathered from her expression the conviction that she would be a cruel stepmother to his children, her mercy that of a loveless noncollector! It should not be. He would do better for them than that. He loved his daughter, but needed not therefore sacrifice his last hopes, if the sacrifice would meet with no acceptance! House and land should be hers, but not his jewels, not the contents of his closet!

Chapter 28.

THE WILL

George came again to see the laird the next day, and had again a
long conference with him. The laird told him that he had fully
resolved to leave everything to his daughter, personal as well as
real, on the one condition that she should marry her cousin; if
she would not, then the contents of his closet, with his library
and certain other articles, should pass to Crawford.

"And you must take care," he said, "if my death should come
suddenly, that anything valuable in this room be carried into
the closet before it is sealed up."

Shrinking as he did from the idea of death, the old man was
yet able, in the interest of his possessions, to talk of it! It was as
if he thought the sole consolation that his things could have in the
loss of their owner was the continuance of their union with each
other, in the heaven of his Mammon-besotted imagination.

George responded heartily, showing a gratitude more genuine than fine, but every virtue partakes of the ground in which
it is grown. He assured the laird that, valuable as was in itself
his contingent gift, which no man could appreciate more than
he, it would be far more valuable to him if it sealed his adop-
tion as his son-in-law. He would rather owe the possession of
the wonderful collection to the daughter than to the father! In
either case the precious property would be held as for him,
each thing as carefully tended as by the laird's own eye and
hand!

Whether it would at the moment have comforted the dying

143

man to be assured, as George might have assured him, that there would be nothing left of him to grieve at the loss of his idols, nothing left of him but a memory to last so long as George and Alexa and one or two more should remain unburied, I cannot tell. It was in any case a dreary outlook for him. Hope and faith and almost love had been sucked from his life by the hindering knotgrass which had spread its white bloodless roots in all directions through soul and heart and mind, exhausting and choking in them everything of divinest origin. The weeds in George's heart were of another kind, nor better nor worse in themselves; the misery was that neither of them was endeavoring to root them out. The thief who is trying to be better is ages ahead of the most honorable man who is making no such effort. The one is alive; the other is dead, and on the way to corruption.

They treated themselves to a gaze together on the cup and the watch; then George put them both away and went to give direction to the laird's lawyer for the drawing up of his new will.

The next day it was brought, read, signed by the laird, and his signature duly witnessed.

Dawtie, being on the spot, was made one of the witnesses. The laird trembled lest her fanaticism should break out in appeal to the lawyer concerning the cup; he could not understand that the cup was nothing to her—that she did not imagine herself a setter-right of wrongs, but knew herself her neighbor's keeper, one that had to deliver his soul from death. Had the cup come into her possession, she would have sent it back to the owner, but it was not worth her care that the Earl of Borland should cast his eyes whenever he wished upon a jewel in a cabinet!

Dawtie was very white as the laird signed his name. Where the others saw but a legal ceremony, she feared her loved master was assigning his soul to the devil, as she had read of Dr. Faustus[25] in the old ballad. He was gliding away into the dark, and no one to whom he had done a good turn with the Mammon of unrighteousness was waiting to receive him into an everlasting habitation! She needed no special cause to love her master, any more than to love the chickens and the calves; she loved because something that could be loved was there present to her. But he had always spoken kindly to her, and had been pleased with her endeavor to serve him. Now he was going where she could do nothing for him except to pray, as her heart and Andrew had taught her, knowing that "all live unto *Him*." But alas, what were prayers where the man would not take the things he prayed for? Nevertheless all things *were* possible with God, and she would pray for him!

It was with white face and trembling hand that she signed her own name, for she felt as if she were giving him a push down the icy slope into the abyss.

But when the thing was done, the old man went quietly to sleep and dreamed of a radiant jewel, glorious as he had never seen jewel before, ever within yet ever eluding his grasp.

Chapter 29.

THE SANGREAL

The next day the laird seemed better, and Alexa began to hope again. But in the afternoon his pulse began to sink, and when Crawford came, the laird could welcome him only with a smile, and a vain effort to put out his hand. George bent down to him. The others, at a sign from his eyes, left the room.

"I can't find it, George!" he whispered.

"I put it away for you last night, you remember," answered George.

"Oh, no, you didn't! I had it in my hand a minute ago! But I fell into a doze, and it is gone! George, get it! Get it for me, or I shall go mad."

George went and brought it to him.

"Thank you! Thank you! Now I remember! I thought I was in hell, and they took it from me!"

"Don't you be afraid, sir! Fall asleep when you feel inclined. I will keep my eye on the cup."

"You will not go away?"

"No. I will stay as long as you like; there is nothing to take me away. If I had thought you would be worse, I would not have gone last night."

"I'm not worse! What put that in your head? Don't you hear me speaking better? I've thought about it, George, and am convinced the cup is a talisman! I am better all the time I hold it! It was because I let you put it away that I was worse last night—for no other reason. If it were not a talisman, how else

146

could it have so nestled itself into my heart? I feel better, always, the moment I take it in my hand. There is something more than common about that chalice! George, what if it should be the Holy Grail?"[26]

He said it with bated breath, and a great white awe upon his countenance. His eyes were shining, and his breath came and went fast. Slowly his aged cheeks flushed with two bright spots. He looked as if the joy of his life was come.

"What if it should be the Holy Grail?" he repeated, and fell asleep with the words on his lips. As the evening deepened into night, he woke. Crawford, sitting beside the bed, saw that a change had come over him. He stared at George as if he could not make him out, closed his eyes, opened them, stared, and again closed them. He seemed to think he was there for no good.

"Would you like me to call Alexa?" said George.

"Call Dawtie—call Dawtie!" he replied.

George rose to go and call her.

"Beware of her!" said the laird, with glazed eyes. "Beware of Dawtie!"

"How?" asked George.

"Beware of her," he repeated. "If she can get the cup, she will! She would take it from me now, if she dared! She will steal it yet! Call Dawtie, call Dawtie!"

Alexa was in the drawing room, on the other side of the hall. George went and told her that her father wanted Dawtie.

"I will find her," she said, and rose, but turned and asked, "How does he seem now?"

"Rather worse," George answered.

"Are you going to be with him through the night?"

"I am. He insists on my staying with him," replied George, almost apologetically.

"Then," she returned, "you must have some supper. We will go down and send up Dawtie."

He followed her to the kitchen. Dawtie was not there, but her mistress found her.

When she entered her master's room, he lay motionless, white with the whiteness of what is dead.

She got brandy and made him swallow some. As soon as he recovered a little, he began to talk wildly.

"O Agnes!" he cried. "Do not leave me. I'm not a bad man! I'm not what Dawtie calls me. I believe in the atonement; I put no trust in myself; my righteousness is as filthy rags. Take me with you. I will go with you. There! Slip that under your white robe—washed in the blood of the Lamb. That will hide it with the rest of my sins! The unbelieving husband is sanctified by the believing wife. Take it, take it! I should be lost in heaven without it! I can't see what I've got on, but it must be the robe of His righteousness, for I have none of my own! What should I be without it! It's all I've got! I couldn't bring away a single thing besides—and it's so cold to have but one thing on—I mean one thing in your hands. Do you say they will make me sell it? That would be worse than coming without it!"

He was talking to his wife, persuading her to smuggle the cup into heaven. Dawtie went on her knees behind the curtain, and began to pray for him all she could. But something seemed stopping her, making her prayer come only from her lips.

"Ah," said the voice of her master. "I thought so! How could I go up, and you praying against me like that? Cup or no cup, the thing was impossible!"

Dawtie opened her eyes—and there he was, holding back the curtain and looking round the edge of it with a face of eagerness, effort, and hate, as of one struggling to go, and unable to break away.

She rose to her feet.

"You are a fiend!" he cried. "I *will* go with Agnes!"

He gave a cry, and ceased, and all was still. They heard the cry in the kitchen and came running up. They found Dawtie bending over her master, with a scared face. He seemed to have struck her, for one cheek was marked with red streaks across its whiteness.

"The Grail! The Holy Grail!" he cried. "I found it! I was bringing it home! She took it from me! She wants it so—"

His jaw fell, and he was dead. Alexa threw herself beside the body. George would have raised her, but she resisted and lay motionless. He stood behind her, watching an opportunity to get the cup from under the bedclothes that he might put it in the closet.

He ordered Dawtie to fetch water for her mistress, but Alexa told her that she did not want any. Once and again George tried to raise her, to get his hand under the bedclothes to feel for the cup.

"He is not dead!" cried Alexa. "He moved!"

"Get some brandy," said George.

She rose, and went to the table for the brandy. George, with the pretense of feeling the dead man's heart, threw back the clothes. He could find no cup. It had fallen farther down! He would wait!

Alexa lifted her father's head on her arm, but it was plain that brandy could not help. She went and sat on a chair away from the bed, hopeless and exhausted. George lifted the clothes from the foot of the bed, then from the farther side and then from the nearer, without attracting her attention. The cup was nowhere to be seen! He put his hand under the body, but the cup was not there! He had to leave the room that Dawtie and Meg might prepare it for burial. Alexa went to her chamber.

A moment after, George returned, called Meg to the door, and said, "There must be a brass cup in the bed somewhere! I brought it to amuse him. He was fond of odd things, you know! If you should find it—"

"I will take care of it," answered Meg, and turned from him curtly.

George felt he had not a friend in the house, and that he must leave things as they were! The door of the closet was locked, and he could not go again to the death chamber to take the laird's keys from the head of the bed. He knew that the two women would not let him. It had been an oversight not to secure them! He was glad the watch was safe, that he had put in the closet; but it mattered little when the cup was missing! He went to the stable, got out his horse, and rode home in the still gray of the midsummer night.

The stillness and the night seemed thinking to each other. George had little imagination, but what he had awoke in him now as he rode slowly along. Step for step the old man seemed following him on silent churchyard feet, through the eerie whiteness of the night. There was neither cloud nor moon, only stars above and around, and a great cold crack in the northeast. He was crying after him, in a voice he could not make him hear! Was he not struggling to warn him not to come into like condemnation? The voice seemed trying to say, "I know now! I know now! I would not believe, but I know now! Give back the cup—give it back!"

George did not allow to himself that there was anything there. It was but a vague movement in that commonplace, unmysterious region, his mind! He heard nothing, positively nothing, with his ears—therefore there was nothing! It was as if one were saying the words, but in reality they came only as a thought rising, continually rising, in his mind! It was but a thought-sound, and no speech, "I know now! I know now! Give it back; give the cup back!" He did not ask himself how the thought came; he cast it away as only an insignificant thing, a thought; he cast it away nonetheless that he found himself answering it, "I can't give it back; I can't find it! Where did you put it? You must have taken it with you!"

"What rubbish!" he said to himself ten times, waking up. "Of course Dawtie took it! Didn't the poor old fellow warn me to beware of her? Nobody but her was in the room when we ran in and found him at the point of death! Where did you put it? I can't find it! I can't give it back!"

He went over in his mind all that had taken place. The laird had the cup when he left him to call Dawtie, and when they came it was nowhere! He was convinced the girl had secured it—in obedience, doubtless, to the instruction of her director, Andrew, ambitious to do justice and curry favor by restoring it! But he could do nothing till the will was read. Was it possible Lexy had put it away? No! She had not had the opportunity.

Chapter 30.

GEORGE AND THE GOLDEN GOBLET

With slow-pacing shadows, the hot hours crept athwart the heath and the house and the dead, and carried the living with them in their invisible current. There is no tide in time; it is a steady current, not returning. Happy they whom it bears inward to the center of things! Alas for those it carries outward to "the flaming walls of creation"! The poor old laird, with all his refinement, all his education, all his interest in philology, prosody, history, and reliquial humanity, had become the slave of a goblet, had left it behind him, had faced the empty universe empty-handed and vanished with a shadow-goblet in his heart; the eyes that gloated over the gems had gone to help the grass to grow.

But the will of the dead remained to trouble for a time the living, for it put his daughter in a painful predicament—until Crawford's property was removed from the house, it would give him constant opportunity of prosecuting the love suit which Alexa had reason to think he intended to resume, and the thought of which had become insupportable to her.

Great was her astonishment when she learned to what the door in the study led, and what a multitude of curious and valuable things were there, of whose presence in the house she had never dreamed. She would gladly have had them for herself, and it pained her to the heart to think of the disappointment of the poor ghost when he saw, if he could see, his treasured hoard emptied out of its hidden and safe abode. For,

151

even if George should magnanimously protest that he did not care for the things enough to claim them, and beg that they might remain where they were, she could not grant his request, for it would be to accept them from him. Had her father left them to her, she would have kept them as carefully as even he could desire—with this difference only, that she would not have shut them up from giving pleasure to others.

She was growing to care more about the truth—gradually coming to see that much she had taken for a more liberal creed was but the same falsehoods in weaker forms, less repulsive only to a mind indifferent to the paramount claims of God on His child. She saw something of the falseness and folly of attempting to recommend religion as not so difficult, so exclusive, so full of prohibition as our ancestors believed it. She saw that although Andrew might regard some things as freely given which others thought God forbade, yet he insisted on what was infinitely higher than the abandonment of everything pleasant—the abnegation, namely, of the very self, and the reception of God instead. With all her supposed progress, she had hitherto been only a recipient of the traditions of the elders! There must be a deeper something—the real religion! She did not yet see that the will of God lay in another direction altogether than the heartiest reception of dogma; that God was too great and too generous to care about anything except righteousness, and only wanted us to be good children; that even honesty was but the path toward righteousness, a condition so pure that honesty itself would nevermore be an object of thought!

She pondered much about her father, and would find herself praying for him, careless of what she had been taught. She could not blind herself to what she knew. He had not been a bad man, as men count badness; but could she in common sense think him a glorified saint, singing in white robes? The polite, kind old man! Her own father! Could she, on the other hand, believe him in flames forever? If so, what a religion was that which required her to believe it, and at the same time to rejoice in the Lord always!

She longed for something positive to believe, something in accordance with which she might work her feelings. She was still on the outlook for definite intellectual formulae to hold. Her dialogues with Andrew had as yet failed to open her eyes to the fact that the faith required of us is faith in a Person, and not in the truest of statements concerning anything, even concerning Him; or to the fact that the very essence of faith in the Living One consists in obedience to Him. A man can obey before he is sure; and except he obey the command he knows to be right, wherever it may come from, he will never be sure. To find the truth, man or woman must be true. She much desired another talk with Andrew.

Persuading himself that Alexa's former feeling toward him must in her trouble reassert itself, and confident that he would find her loath to part with her father's wonderful collection, George waited the effect of the will. After the reading of it, he had gone away directly, that his presence might not add to the irritation which he concluded it must cause in her, even in the midst of her sorrow. But at the end of a week he wrote, saying that he felt it his duty, if only in gratitude to his friend, to inform himself as to the attention the valuable things he had left him might require. He assured Alexa that he had done nothing to influence her father in the matter, and much regretted the awkward position in which his will had placed both her and him. At the same time it was not unnatural that he should wish such precious objects to be possessed by one who would care for them as he had himself cared for them. He hoped, therefore, that she would allow him access to her father's rooms. He would not, she might rest assured, intrude himself upon her sorrow, though he would be compelled to ask her before long, whether he might hope that her father's wish would have any influence in reviving the favor which had once been the joy of his life.

Alexa saw that if she consented to see him, he would take it as a permission to press his claim, and the idea was not to be borne. She wrote him therefore a stiff letter, telling him the house was at his service, but he must excuse her.

The next morning brought him early to Potlurg. The cause of his haste was his uneasiness about the chalice.

Old Meg opened the door to him, and he followed her straight into the drawing room. Alexa was there, and far from expecting him. Yet, annoyed at his appearance as she was, she found his manner and behavior less unpleasant than at any time since his return. He was gentle and self-restrained, assuming no familiarity beyond that of a distant relative, and giving the impression of having come against his will and only from a sense of duty.

"Did you not have my note?" she asked.

He had hoped, he said, to save her the trouble of writing.

She handed him her father's bunch of keys, and left the room. George went to the laird's closet, and having spent an hour in it, again sought Alexa. The wonderful watch was in his hand.

"I feel the more pleasure, Alexa," he said, "in begging you to accept this trinket, that it was the last addition to your dear father's collection. I had myself the good fortune to please him with it a few days before his death."

"No, thank you, George," returned Alexa. "It is a beautiful thing—my father showed it to me—but I cannot take it."

"It was more of you than him I thought when I purchased it, Alexa. You know why I could not offer it to you!"

"The same reason exists now."

"I am sorry to have to force myself on your attention, but—"

"Dawtie!" cried Alexa.

Dawtie came running.

"Wait a minute, Dawtie. I will speak to you presently," said her mistress.

George rose. He had laid the watch on the table, and seemed to have forgotten it.

"Please take the watch with you," said Alexa.

"Certainly, if you wish it!" he answered.

"And my father's keys too," she added.

"Will you not be kind enough to take charge of them?"

"I would rather not be accountable for anything under them. No, you must take the keys!"

"I cannot help regretting," said George, "that your honored father should have thought fit to lay this burden of possession upon me."

Alexa made no answer.

"I comforted myself with the hope that you would feel them as much your own as ever!" he resumed, in a tone of disappointment and dejection.

"I did not know of their existence before I knew they were

never to be mine."

"Never, Alexa?"

"Never."

George walked to the door, but there turned and said, "By the way, you know that cup your father was so fond of?"

"No."

"Not that gold cup set with stones?"

"I saw something in his hands once, in bed, that might have been a cup."

"It is a thing of great value—of pure gold, and every stone in it a gem."

"Indeed!" returned Alexa with a marked indifference.

"Yes, it was the work of the famous Benvenuto Cellini, made for Pope Clement the Seventh, for his own Communion cup. Your father priced it at three thousand pounds. In his last moments, when his mind was wandering, he fancied it the Holy Grail. He had it in the bed with him when he died. That I know!"

"And it is missing?"

"Perhaps Dawtie could tell us what has become of it! She was with the laird last!"

Dawtie, who had stood aside to let him pass to the open door, looked up with a flash in her eyes, but said nothing.

"Have you seen the cup, Dawtie?" asked her mistress.

"No, ma'am."

"Do you know it?"

"Very well, ma'am."

"Then you don't know what has become of it?"

"No, ma'am. I know nothing about it."

"Take care, Dawtie!" said George. "This is a matter that will have to be searched into."

"When did you last see it, Dawtie?" inquired Alexa.

"The very day my master died, ma'am. He was looking at it, but when he saw I saw him, he took it inside the bedclothes."

"And you have not seen it since?"

"No, ma'am."

"And you do not know where it is?" said George.

"No, sir. How should I?"

"You never touched it?"

"I canna say that, sir. I brought it him from his closet when he sent me for it."

"What do you think may have become of it?"

"I dinna know, sir."

"Would you allow me to make a thorough search in the place where it was last seen?" asked George, turning to his cousin.

"By all means. Dawtie, go help Mr. Crawford to look."

"Please, ma'am, it canna be there! We've had the carpet up, and the floor scrubbed. There's not a hole or a corner we havena been into, and that was yesterday!"

"We must find it!" said George. "It must be in the house!"

"It must, sir!" said Dawtie.

But George more than doubted it. "I do believe," he said, "the laird would rather have lost his whole collection!"

"Indeed, sir, I think he would!"

"Then you have talked to him about it?"

"Yes, I have, sir," answered Dawtie, sorry she had brought out the question.

"And you know the worth of the thing?"

"Yes, sir—that is, I dinna know how much it was worth, but I should say pounds and pounds!"

"Then, Dawtie, I must ask you again, where is it?"

"I know nothing about it, sir. I wish I did!"

"Why do you wish you did?"

"Because—" began Dawtie, and stopped short. She shrank from impugning the honesty of the dead man, and in the presence of his daughter.

"It looks a little fishy, doesn't it, Dawtie? Why not speak straight out? Perhaps you would not mind searching Meg's trunk for me! She may have taken it for a bit of old brass, you know!"

"I will answer for my servants, Mr. Crawford!" said Alexa. "I will not have Meg's box searched."

"It is desirable to get rid of any suspicion," replied George.

"I have none," returned Alexa.

George was silent.

"I will ask Meg, if you like, sir," said Dawtie, "but I am sure it will be no use. A servant in this house soon learns not to go by the look of things. We dinna treat anything here as if we knew all about it!"

"When did you see the goblet first?" persisted George.

156

"Goblet, sir? I thought you were speaking of the gold cup!"
By *goblet* Dawtie understood a small iron pot.

"Goblet, or cup, or chalice—whatever you like to call it—I ask
you how you came to know about it!"

"I know very little about it."

"It is plain you know more than you care to tell. If you will
not answer me, you will have to answer a magistrate."

"Then I will answer a magistrate!" said Dawtie, beginning to
grow angry.

"You had better answer me, Dawtie! It will be easier for you.
What do you know about the cup?"

"I know it wasna master's, and isna yours—really and truly."

"What can have put such a lie in your head?"

"If it be a lie, sir, it is told in plain print."

"Where?"

But Dawtie judged it time to stop. She bethought herself that
she would not have said so much had she not been angry.

"Sir," she answered, "you have been asking me questions all
this time, and I have been answering them; it is your turn to
answer me one."

"If I see proper."

"Did my old master tell you the history of that cup?"

"I do not choose to answer the question."

"Very well, sir."

Dawtie turned to leave the room.

"Stop! Stop!" cried Crawford. "I have not done with you yet,
my girl! You have not told me what you meant when you said
the cup did not belong to the laird!"

"I dinna choose to answer the question," said Dawtie.

"Then you shall answer to a magistrate!"

"I will, sir," she replied, and stood.

Crawford left the room, and rode home in a rage. Dawtie
went about her work with a bright spot on each cheek, indignant at the man's rudeness, but praying God to take her heart
in His hand, and cool the fever of it. The words rose in her
mind, "It must needs be that offenses come, but woe unto that
man by whom they come!"

She was at once filled with pity for the man who could side
with the wrong, and want everything his own way; for, sooner
or later, confusion must be his portion. The Lord had said,

"There is nothing covered that shall not be revealed, neither hid that shall not be known!"

"He needs to be shamed," she said, "but he is Thy child; care for him too."

George felt that he had not borne a dignified part, and knew that his last chance with Alexa was gone. Then he too felt the situation unendurable, and set about removing his property. He wrote to Alexa that he could no longer doubt it her wish to be rid of the collection, and able to use the room. It was desirable also, he said, that a thorough search should be made in those rooms before he placed the matter of the missing cup in the hands of the magistrates.

Dawtie's last words had sufficed to remove any lingering doubt as to what had become of the chalice. It did not occur to him that one so anxious to do the justice of restoration would hardly be capable of telling lies, of defiling her soul that a bit of property might be recovered; he took it for granted that she meant to be liberally rewarded by the earl.

George would have ill understood the distinction Dawtie made—that the body of the cup *might* belong to him, but the soul of the cup *did* belong to another; or her assertion that where the soul was, there the body ought to be; or her belief that he who had the soul had the right to ransom the body. It was all reasoning possible only to a childlike nature; she had pondered to find the true law of the case, and this was her conclusion.

George suspected, and grew convinced, that Alexa was a party to the abstraction of the cup. She had, he said, begun to share in the extravagant notions of a group of pietists whose leader was that detestable fellow, Ingram. Alexa was attached to Dawtie, and Dawtie was one of them. He believed Alexa would do anything to spite him. To bring trouble on Dawtie would be to punish her mistress, and that pious farmer too!

Chapter 31

THE PROSECUTION

Crawford took his things away from Potlurg, and satisfied himself that the cup was nowhere among them. He directly made a statement of the case to a magistrate he knew, and so represented it as the outcome of the hypocrisy of pietism that the magistrate, hating everything called fanatical, at once granted him a warrant to apprehend Dawtie on the charge of theft.

It was a terrible shock when they came for her. Alexa cried out with indignation. Dawtie turned white and then red, but uttered never a word.

"Dawtie," said her mistress, "tell me what you know about the cup. You do know something that you have not told me!"

"I do, ma'am, but I willna tell it except I am forced."

"That you are going to be, my poor girl! I am very sorry, for I am perfectly sure you have done nothing you know to be wrong!"

"I have done nothing you or anybody would think wrong, ma'am."

She put on her Sunday frock, and went down to go with the policeman. To her joy she found her mistress at the door, ready to accompany her. They had two miles or more to walk, but that was nothing to either.

Questioned by the magistrate, not unkindly, for her mistress was there, Dawtie told everything—how first she came upon the likeness and history of the cup, and then saw the cup itself in her master's hands.

Crawford told how the laird had warned him against Dawtie, giving him to understand that she had been seized with a passion for the goblet such that she would peril her soul to possess it, and that he dared not let her know where it was.

"Sir," said Dawtie, "he couldna have distrusted me like that, for he gave me his keys, and sent me to fetch the cup when he was too ill to go to it."

"If that be true, your worship," said Crawford, "it does not affect the fact that the cup was in the hands of the old man when I left him and she went to him, and from that moment it has not been seen."

"Did he have it when you went to him?" asked the magistrate.

"I didna see it, sir. He was in a kind of faint when I got up."

Crawford said that, hearing a cry, he ran up again, and found the old man at the point of death, with just strength to cry out before he died, that Dawtie had taken the cup from him. Dawtie was leaning over him, but he had not imagined the accusation more than the delirious fancy of a dying man, till it appeared that the cup was not to be found.

The magistrate made out Dawtie's commitment for trial. He remarked that she might have been misled by a false notion of duty; he had been informed that she belonged to a sect claiming the right to think for themselves on the profoundest mysteries—and here was the result!

There was not a man in Scotland less capable of knowing what any woman was thinking, or more incapable of doubting his own insight.

Doubtless, he went on, she had superstitiously regarded the cup as exercising a satanic influence on the mind of her master; but even if she confessed it now, he must make an example of one whose fanaticism would set wrong right after the notions of an illiterate sect, and not according to the laws of the land. He must send the case to be tried by a jury! If she convinced the twelve men composing that jury of the innocence she protested, she would then be a free woman!

Dawtie stood very white all the time he was speaking, and her lips every now and then quivered as if she were going to cry, but she did not. Alexa offered bail, but his worship would not accept it; his righteous soul was too indignant. She went to Dawtie and kissed her, and together they followed the policeman to the door, where Dawtie was to get into a spring cart with him, and be driven to the county town, there to lie waiting the assizes.[27]

The bad news had spread so fast that as they came out, up came Andrew. At sight of him, Dawtie gently laughed, like a pleased child. The policeman who, like many present, had been prejudiced by her looks in her favor, dropped behind, and she walked between her mistress and Andrew to the cart.

"Dawtie!" said Andrew.

"O An'rew! Has God forgotten me?" she returned, stopping short.

"For God to forget," answered Andrew, "would not to be God any longer."

"But here I am on my road to a prison, An'rew! I didna think He would have let them do it!"

"A bairn might just as well say—when its nurse lays it into its cradle, and says, 'Now, lie still!'—'Mammy, I didna think ye would have let her do it!' He's all about ye and in ye, Dawtie, and this is come to ye just to let ye know that He is. He raised ye up just to spend His glory upon! I say, Dawtie, did Jesus Christ deserve what He got?"

"No one bit, An'rew! What for should ye ask such a thing?"

"Then do ye think God had forgotten Him?"

"Maybe He thought it just for a minute!"

"Well, ye have thought just for a minute, and ye must think it no more."

"But God couldna forget *Him*, An'rew; He got it all for doing His will!"

"Evil may come upon us from other causes than doing the will of God; but from whatever cause it comes, the thing we have to see to is, that through it all we do the will of God!"

"What's His will now, An'rew?"

"That ye take it quietly. Shall not the Father do with His own child what He will? Can He no shift it from the one arm to the other, but that the bairn must cry? He has ye, Dawtie! It's all right!"

"Though He slay me, yet will I trust in Him!" said Dawtie.

She raised her head. The color had come back to her face, and her lip had ceased to tremble. She stepped on steadily to where, a few yards from the door, the spring cart was waiting

161

her. She bade her mistress good-bye, then turned to Andrew and said, "Good-bye, An'rew! I am not afraid."

"I am going with you, Dawtie," said Andrew.

"No, sir, you can't do that!" said the policeman. "At least, you can't go in the cart!"

"No, no, An'rew!" cried Dawtie. "I would rather go alone. I am quite happy now. God will do with me as He pleases."

"I am going with you," said Alexa, "if the policeman will let me."

"Oh, yes, ma'am! A lady's different! I've got to account for the prisoner, you see, sir!"

"I don't think you should, ma'am," said Dawtie. "It's a long way!"

"I am going," returned her mistress decisively.

"God bless you, ma'am!" said Andrew.

Alexa had heard what he said to Dawtie, and a new light had broken upon her. "God is like that, is He!" she said to herself. "You can go close up to Him whenever you like."

Chapter 32.

A TALK AT POTLURG

It would be three weeks before the assizes came. The house of Potlurg was searched by the police from garret to cellar, but in vain; the cup was not found.

As soon as the law gave up searching, Alexa had the old door of the laird's closet reopened and the room cleaned. Almost unfurnished as it was, she made of it her sitting parlor. But often her work or her book would lie on her lap, and she would find herself praying for the dear father for whom she could do nothing else now, but for whom she might have done so much, had she been like Dawtie. Her servant had cared for her father more than she had!

As she sat there one morning alone, brooding a little, thinking a little, reading a little, and praying through it all, Meg appeared and said Mister Andrew wanted to see her. He had called more than once to inquire after Dawtie, but had not before asked to see her mistress.

Alexa felt herself unaccountably agitated. When he walked into the room, however, she was able to receive him quietly. He came, he said, to ask when she had seen Dawtie. He would have gone himself to see her, but his father was ailing, and he had double work to do. Besides, Dawtie did not seem willing to see him! Alexa told him she had been with her the day before, and had found her a little pale, and, she feared, rather troubled in her mind. Dawtie had said she would trust God to the last, but confessed herself assailed by doubts.

163

"I said to her," continued Alexa, " 'Be sure, Dawtie, God will make your innocence known one day!'

"She answered, 'Of course, ma'am, there is nothing hidden that shallna be unknown, but I am not impatient about that. The Jews to this day think Jesus an impostor!'

" 'But surely,' said I, 'you care that people should understand you are no thief, Dawtie!'

" 'Yes, I do,' she answered. 'All I say is that it doesna trouble me. I want only to be downright sure that God is looking after me all the time. I am willing to sit in prison till I die, if He pleases.'

" 'God can't please that!' I said.

" 'If He doesna care to take me out, I dinna care to go out,' said Dawtie. 'It's not that I'm good; it's only that I dinna care for anything He doesna care for. What would it be that all men acquitted me, if God didna trouble Himself about His children?' "

"You see, ma'am, it comes to this," said Andrew. "It is God Dawtie cares about, not herself! If God is all right, Dawtie is all right. The *if* sometimes takes one shape, sometimes another, but the fear is the same—and the very fear is faith. Sometimes the fear is that there may be no God, and that you might call a fear for herself; but when Dawtie fears lest God should not be caring for her, that is a fear for God; for if God did not care for His creature, He would be no true God!"

"Then He could not exist!"

"True! And so you are back on the other fear."

"What would you have said to her, Mr. Ingram?"

"I would have reminded her that Jesus was perfectly content with His Father; that He knew what was coming upon Himself, and never doubted Him—just gloried that His Father was what He knew Him to be."

"I see! But what did you mean when you said that Dawtie's very fear was faith?"

"Think, ma'am—people that only care to be saved, that is, not to be punished for their sins, are anxious only about themselves, not about God and His glory at all. They talk about the glory of God, but they make it consist in our selfishness. According to them, He seeks everything for Himself; which is dead against the truth of God, a diabolic slander of God. It does not trouble them to believe such things about God; they do not even desire that God should not be like that—they only want to escape Him. They dare not say God will not do this or that, however clear it be that it would not be fair: they are in terror of contradicting the Bible. They make more of the Bible than of God, and so fail to find the truth of the Bible, and accept things concerning God which are not in the Bible, and are the greatest of insults to Him!

"Dawtie never thinks about saving her soul; she has no fear about her soul; she is only anxious about God and His glory. How the doubts come, God knows; but if she did not love God, they would not be there. Jesus says God will speedily avenge His elect—those that cry day and night to Him—which I take to mean that He will soon save them from all such miseries. Free Dawtie from unsureness about God, and she has no fear left. All is well, in the prison or on the throne of God, if He only be what she thinks He is. If anyone says that doubt cannot coexist with faith, I answer, it can with love, and love is the greater of the two, yes, is the very heart of faith itself. God's children are not yet God's men and women. The God that many people believe in, claiming to be *the* religious ones because they believe in Him, is a God not worth believing in, a God that ought not to be believed in. The life given by such a God would be a life not worth living, even if He made His votaries as happy as they would choose to be. A God like that could not make a woman like Dawtie anxious about Him! If God be not such as Jesus, what good would the proving of her innocence be to Dawtie? A mighty thing indeed that the world should confess she was not a thief! But to know that there is a perfect God, one for us to love with all the power of love of which we feel we are capable, is worth going out of existence for; while to know God Himself is to make every throb of consciousness a divine ecstasy!"

Andrew's heart was full, and out of its fullness he spoke. Never before had he been able in the presence of Alexa to speak as he felt. Never before had he had any impulse to speak as now. As soon would he have gone to sow seed on a bare rock as sow words of spirit and life in her ears!

"I am beginning to understand you," she said. "Will you forgive me? I have been very self-confident and conceited! What a mercy things are not as I thought they were—thought they ought to be!"

"And the glory of the Lord shall cover the earth as the waters cover the sea!" said Andrew. "And men's hearts shall be full of bliss, because they have found their Father, and He is what He is, and they are going home to Him."

He rose.

"You will come and see me again soon, will you not?" Alexa asked.

"As often as you please, ma'am. I am your servant."

"Then come tomorrow."

He went on the morrow, and the next day, and the day after—almost every day while Dawtie was waiting her trial.

Almost every morning Alexa went by train to see Dawtie; and the news she brought back to Andrew, Andrew would carry to the girl's parents. Dawtie continued unwilling to see Andrew; he had had trouble enough with her already, she said. Yet Andrew could not quite understand her refusal.

Chapter 33.

A GREAT OFFERING

Two days before the assizes, Andrew was with Alexa in her parlor. It was a cool autumn evening, and she proposed they should go up on the heath, which came close to the back of the house.

When they reached the top of the hill, a cold wind was blowing, and Andrew, full of care for old and young, man and woman, made Alexa draw her shawl closer about her throat, where, with his rough plowman hands, he pinned it for her. She saw, felt, and noted his hands; a pitying admiration, of which only the pity was foolish, woke in her; and ere she knew, she was looking up in his face with such a light in her eyes that Andrew found himself embarrassed, and let his own eyes fall. Moved by that sense of class superiority which has no place in the kingdom of heaven, she attributed his modesty to self-depreciation. And then the conviction rose in her, which has often risen in such as she, that there is a magnanimity demanding the sacrifice, not merely of conventional dignity, but of conventional propriety. She felt that a great lady, to be more great, must stoop; that it was her part to make the approach which, between equals, was the part of the man; that the patroness must do what the woman might not. This man was worthy of any woman; and he should not, because of the humility that dared not presume, fail of what he deserved!

"Andrew," she said, "I am going to do an unusual thing, but you are not like other men, and will not misunderstand! I know you now—know you to be as far above other men as the clouds are above this heath!"

"Oh, no, no, ma'am!" protested Andrew.

"Hear me out, Andrew," then paused a little. "Tell me," she resumed, "ought we not to love the best we know?"

"Surely, ma'am!" he answered, uncomfortable, but not anticipating what was on the way.

"Andrew, you are the best I know. I have said it! I do not care what the world thinks, for you are more to me than all the worlds! If you will take me, I am yours."

She looked him in the face with the feeling that she had done a brave and a right thing.

Andrew stood stock still. "*Me*, ma'am!" he gasped, and grew pale, then red as a foggy sun. But he made scarcely a moment's pause. "It's a godlike thing you have done, ma'am!" he said. "But I cannot make the return it deserves. From the heart of my heart I thank you. I can say no more." His voice trembled, and he turned away to conceal his emotion.

She stifled a sob, but then came her greatness indeed to the front. Instead of drawing herself up with the bitter pride of a woman whose best is scorned, Alexa behaved divinely. She went close to Andrew, laid her hand on his arm, and said, "Forgive me, Andrew. I made a mistake. I had no right to make it. Do not be grieved, I beg. You are nowise to blame. Let us continue friends."

"Thank you, ma'am!" said Andrew, in a tone of deepest gratitude, and said not a word more. They walked side by side back to the house.

Said Alexa to herself, "I have at least been refused by a man worthy of the honor I did him! I made no mistake in him!"

When they reached the door, she stopped. Andrew took off his hat, and said, holding it in his hand as he spoke, "Good night, ma'am! You will send for me if you want me?"

"I will. Good night!" said Alexa, and went with a strange weight upon her heart.

Shut in her room, she wept sorely, but not bitterly; and the next day old Meg, at least, saw no change in her.

Said Andrew to himself, "I will be her servant always." He was humbled, not uplifted.

168

Chapter 34.

A GREATER OFFERING

The next evening, that before the trial, Andrew presented himself at the prison and was admitted.

Dawtie came to meet him, held out her hand, and said, "Thank you, An'rew!"

"How are you, Dawtie?"

"Well enough, An'rew!"

"God is with us, Dawtie."

"Are you sure, An'rew?"

"Dawtie, I cannot *see* God's eyes looking at me, but I am ready to do what He wants me to do, and so I feel He is with me."

"O An'rew, I wish I could be sure."

"Let us take the risk together, Dawtie!"

"What risk, An'rew?"

"The risk that makes you not sure, Dawtie—the risk that is at once the worst and the least—the risk that our hope should be in vain, and there is no God. But, Dawtie, there is that in my heart that cries Christ *did* die, and *did* rise again, and God is doing His best. His perfect love is our perfect safety. It is hard upon Him that His own children will not trust Him!"

"If He would but show Himself!"

"The sight of Him would make us believe in Him without knowing Him, and what kind of faith would that be for Him or for us? We should be bad children, taking Him for a weak parent. We must know Him! When we do, there will be no fear, no doubt. We shall run straight home! Dawtie, shall we go together?"

"Yes, surely, An'rew! God knows I try. I'm ready to do whatever you tell me, An'rew!"

"No, Dawtie! You must never do what I tell you, except you think it right."

"Yes, I know that. But I am sure I should think it right."

"We've been of one mind for a long time now, Dawtie."

"Since long before I had any mind of my own!" responded Dawtie.

"Then let us be of one heart too, Dawtie!"

She was so accustomed to hear Andrew speak in figures, that sometimes she looked through and beyond his words. She did so now, and seeing nothing, stood perplexed.

"Willna ye, Dawtie?" said Andrew, holding out his hands.

"I dinna freely understand ye, An'rew!"

"Ye heavenly idiot!" cried Andrew. "Will ye be my wife, or will ye no?"

Dawtie threw her shapely arms above her head, her head fell back, and she seemed to gaze into the unseen. Then she gave a gasp, her arms dropped to her sides, and she would have fallen, had not Andrew taken her.

"An'rew! An'rew!" she sighed, and was still in his arms.

"Willna ye, Dawtie?" he whispered.

"Wait," she murmured. "Wait."

"I willna wait, Dawtie."

"Wait till ye hear what they'll say the morn."

"Dawtie, I'm ashamed of ye! What care I, and what dare ye care what they say! Are ye no the Lord's clean yowie?[28] If ye care for what any man thinks of ye but the Lord Himself, ye're no all His! If ye care for what I think of ye, or of anything nor what He thinks, ye're no so much His as I must have ye before we part company—which, please God, will be on the other side of eternity!"

"But, An'rew, it willna do to say of your father's son that he took a wife from jail!"

"Indeed, they should say nothing other! What other came I for? Would ye have me ashamed of one of God's elect—a lady of the Lord's own court?"

"Eh, but I'm afraid it's all the compassion of your heart, sir! Ye would make up to me for the disgrace! Ye could well do wanting me!"

"I willna say," returned Andrew, "that I couldna live wanting ye, for that would be to say I wasna worth offering to ye; and it would be to deny Him that made you and me for one another; but I would have some sore time! I'll just speak to the minister to be ready the minute the Lord opens yer prison door."

The same moment, in came the governor of the prison with his wife, for they were much interested in Dawtie.

"Sir, and ma'am," said Andrew, "will you please witness that this woman is my wife?"

"It's Master An'rew Ingram of the Knowe," said Dawtie. "He wants me to marry him!"

"I want her to go before the court as my wife," said Andrew. "She would have me wait till the jury said this or that! How can the jury give me my wife—as if I didn't know her!"

"You won't have him, I see!" said Mrs. Innes, turning to Dawtie.

"Have him!" cried Dawtie. "I would have him if there were but the head of him!"

"Then you are husband and wife!" said the governor. "Only you should have the thing done properly by the minister—afterwards."

"I'll see to that, sir!" answered Andrew.

"Come, wife," said the governor, "we must let them have a few minutes alone together."

"There!" said Andrew, when the door closed. "Ye're my wife now, Dawtie! Let them acquit ye or condemn ye, it's you and me now, whatever comes!"

Dawtie broke into a flood of tears—an experience all but new to her—and found it did her good. She smiled as she wiped her eyes, and said, "Well, An'rew, if the Lord hasna appeared in His own likeness to deliver me, He's done the next best thing."

"Dawtie," answered Andrew, "the Lord never does the next best. The thing He does is always better than the thing He does not!"

"Let me think, and I'll try to understand," said Dawtie, but Andrew went on.

"The best thing, when a body's no ready for it, would be the worst thing to give him—and no the thing for the Father of Lights to give! Shortbread might be worse for a half-hungered

171

bairn than a stone! But the minute it's fit we should look upon the face of the Son of man, our own God-born Brother, we'll see Him, Dawtie! We'll see Him! Heart canna think what it'll be like! And now, Dawtie, will ye tell me what for ye wouldna let me come and see ye before?"

"I will, An'rew. I was no sooner left to myself in the prison than I found myself thinking about you—you first, and no the Lord! I said to myself, 'This is awful! I'm leaning upon An'rew, and no upon the First and the Last!' I saw that that was to break away from Him that was nearest me, and trust one that was farther away—which wasna in the holy reason of things. So I said to myself I would meet my fate with the Lord alone, and wouldna have you come between Him and me! Now ye have it, An'rew!"

Andrew took her in his arms, and said, "Thank ye, Dawtie! Eh, but I am content! And you thought you hadna faith! Good night, Dawtie. Ye must go to yer bed, an' grow stout in heart for the morn."

Chapter 35.

THE VERDICT

Through the governor of the jail Andrew obtained permission to stand near the prisoner at the trial. The counsel for the prosecution did all he could, and the counsel for the defense not much—at least Dawtie's friends thought so—and the judge summed up with the greatest impartiality. Dawtie's simplicity and calmness, her confidence devoid of self-assertion, had its influence on the jury, and they gave the uncomfortable verdict of "Not Proven,"[29] so that Dawtie was discharged.

Alexa had a carriage ready to take Dawtie home. As Dawtie went to it, she whispered to her husband, "Ye have to take me wanting a character, An'rew!"

"Jesus went home without a character, and was well received!" said Andrew with a smile. "You'll be over tonight to see the old folk?"

"Yes, Andrew—I'm sure the mistress will let me!"

"Don't say a word to her of our marriage, except she has heard and mentions it. I want to tell her myself. You will find me at the croft when you come, and I will go back with you."

In the evening Dawtie came, and brought the message that her mistress would like to see him.

Later, when Andrew entered the room, Alexa rose to meet him. He stopped short. "I thank you, ma'am," he said, "for your great kindness to Dawtie. We were married in the prison. She is my wife now."

"Married! Your wife?" echoed Alexa, flushing, and drawing

back a step.

"I had loved her long, ma'am, and when trouble came upon her, the time came for me to stand by her side."

"You had not spoken to her then—till—?"

"Not till last night. I said before the governor of the prison and Mrs. Innes that we were husband and wife. If you please, ma'am, we shall have the proper ceremony as soon as possible."

"I wish I had known!" said Alexa almost to herself, with a troubled smile.

"I wish you had, ma'am!" responded Andrew.

She raised her face with a look of confidence. "Will you please to forget, Andrew?"

Nobility had carried the day. She had not one mean thought either of him or the girl.

"To forget is not in man's power, ma'am, but I shall never think a thought you would wish unthought."

She held out her hand to him, and their friendship was sealed forever.

"Will you be married here, Andrew? The house is at your service," she said.

"Don't you think it ought to be at her father's, ma'am?"

"You are right," said Alexa, and she sat down.

Andrew stood in silence, for he saw she was meditating something.

At length, she raised her head, and spoke. "You have been compelled to take the step sooner than you intended, have you not?"

"Yes, ma'am."

"Then you can hardly be so well prepared as you would like to be!"

"We shall manage."

"It will hardly be convenient for your mother, I fear! You have nowhere else to take her—have you?"

"No, ma'am, but my mother loves us both. And," he added simply, "where there's room for me, there's room for her now!"

"Would you mind if I asked how your parents take it?"

"They don't say much, though their dignity is taking a fall. You see, ma'am, we are all proud until we learn that we have one Master, and that we are all brethren. But they will soon get over it."

When I see a man lifting up those that are beneath him, not pulling down those that are above him, I will believe in his ideas of brotherhood. Those who most resent being looked down upon are in general the readiest to look down upon others. It is not principle, it is not truth, it is themselves they regard. Of all false divinities, Self is the most illogical.

"If God had been the mighty monarch they represent Him," continued Andrew, "He would never have let us come near Him."

"Did you hear Mr. Rackstraw's sermon on the condescension of God?" asked Alexa.

"The condescension of God, ma'am! There is no such thing. God never condescended with one Jovelike nod, all His mighty, eternal life! God condescend to His children—their spirits born of His spirit, their hearts the children of His heart? No, ma'am! There never was a falser, uglier word in any lying sermon!"

His eyes flashed and his face shone. Alexa thought she had never seen him look so grand.

"I see!" she answered. "I will never use the word about God again!"

"Thank you, ma'am."

"Why should you thank me?"

"I beg your pardon; I had no right to thank you. But I am so tried with the wicked things said about God by people who think they are speaking to His pleasure and not in His despite, that I am apt to talk foolishly. I don't wonder at God's patience with the wicked, but I do wonder at His patience with the pious!"

"They don't know better!"

"How are they to know better while they are so sure about everything? I would infinitely rather believe in no God at all, than in such a God as they would have me believe in!"

"Oh, but Andrew, I had not a glimmer of what you meant, of what you really objected to, or what you loved! Now, I cannot even recall what it was I did not like in your teaching. I think it was that, instead of listening to know what you meant, I was always thinking how to oppose you, or trying to find out by what name you were to be called. One time I thought you were an Arminian,[30] another time a Socinian,[31] then a Swedenborgian,[32] then an Arian![33] I read a history of the sects of the

175

Middle Ages, just to discover where I could set you down. I told people you did not believe this and you did not believe that, when I knew neither what you believed nor did not believe. I thought I did, but it was all a mistake and imagination. When you would not discuss things with me, I thought you were afraid of losing the argument. Now I see that instead of disputing about opinions, I should have been saying, 'God be merciful to me a sinner!' "

"God be praised!" said Andrew. "Ma'am, you are a free woman! The Father has called you, and you have said, 'Here I am!' "

"I hope so, Andrew, thanks to God by you! But I am forgetting what I wanted to say! Would it not be better—after you are married, I mean—to let Dawtie stay with me a while? I will promise you not to work her too hard," she added, with a little laugh.

"I see, ma'am! It is just like you! You want people to know that you believe in her!"

"Yes, but I want also to do what I can to keep such good tenants. Therefore, I must add a room or two to your house, that there may be good accommodation for you all."

"You make thanks impossible, ma'am! I will speak to Dawtie about it. I know she will be glad not to leave you! I will take care not to trouble the house."

"You shall do just as Dawtie and you please. Where Dawtie is, there will be room for you!"

Already Alexa's pain had grown quite bearable.

Dawtie needed no persuading. She was so rich in the possession of Andrew that she could go a hundred years without seeing him, she said. It was only that he would come and see her now, instead of her going to see him!

In ten days they were married at her father's cottage. Her father and mother then accompanied her and Andrew to the Knowe, to dine with Andrew's father and mother. In the evening the new pair went out for a walk in the old fields.

"It *seems*, Dawtie, as if God were here!" said Andrew.

"I would see Him, An'rew! I would rather *you* went away than God!"

"Suppose He was nowhere, Dawtie?"

"If God werena in *you*, ye wouldna be what ye are to your

176

ignorant Dawtie, An'rew! She needs her Father in heaven more
nor her An'rew! But I'm saying things so true that it's just silly
to say them! Eh, it's like heaven itself to be out of that prison,
and walking about with you! God has given me everything—
just *everything*, An'rew!"

"God was with ye in the prison, Dawtie!"

"Aye! But I like better to be with Him here!"

"And ye may be sure He likes better to have ye here!"
rejoined Andrew.

Chapter 36.

THE FINAL SEARCH

The next day Alexa set Dawtie to search the house yet again for the missing goblet.

"It must be somewhere!" she said. "We are beset with an absolute contradiction—the thing can't be in the house and yet it must be in the house!"

"If we do find it," returned Dawtie, "folk'll say them that could hide would well seek! I shouldna look without you, ma'am!"

The study was bare of books, and the empty shelves gave no hint of concealment. They stood in its dreariness, looking vaguely around them.

"Did it ever come to you, ma'am," said Dawtie, "that a minute or two passed between Mr. Crawford coming down the stair with you, and me going up to the master? When I passed into the room, he lay panting in the bed; but as I brooded upon each thing alone in the prison, he came before me, there in the bed, as if he had gotten out of it, and hidden away the cup, and was just gotten into it again, the same moment I came in."

"Dying people will do strange things!" rejoined her mistress. "But it brings us no nearer the cup!"

"The surer we are, the better we'll seek!" said Dawtie.

They began, and went over the room thoroughly, looking everywhere they could think of. They had all but given it up to go elsewhere when Dawtie, standing again in the middle and looking about in a sort of unconscious hopelessness, found her eyes on the mantelshelf, and went and laid her hand upon it. It was of wood, and she fancied it a little loose, but she could not move it.

"When Andrew comes we'll get him to examine it!" said Alexa.

He came in the evening, and Alexa told him what they had been doing. She begged him to get tools, and see whether there was not a space under the mantelshelf. But Andrew, accustomed to ponder contrivances with Sandy, would have a good look at it first. He came presently upon a clever little spring, pressing which, he could lift the shelf. There under it, sure enough, in rich response to the candle he held, flashed the gems of the curiously wrought chalice of gold! Alexa gave a cry, Andrew drew a deep breath, and Dawtie laughed like a child. They gazed on it, passed it from one to the other, pored over the gems, and over the raised work that enclosed them. They began to talk about what was to be done with it.

"We will send it to the earl!" said Alexa.

"No," said Andrew. "That would be to make ourselves judges in the case! Your father must have paid money for it; he gave it to Mr. Crawford, and Mr. Crawford must not be robbed!"

"Stop, Andrew!" said Alexa. "Everything in the next room and in the library was left to my cousin; whatever else was left him was individually described. The cup was not in the next room, and was not mentioned. Providence has left us to do with it as we may judge right. I think it ought to be taken to Borland Hall—and by Dawtie."

"Well! She will mention that your father bought it?"

"I will not take a shilling for it!"

"Is not that because you are not quite sure you have the right to dispose of it?"

"I would not take the price of it if my father had left the cup expressly to me!"

"Had he done so, you would have a right to what he paid for it. To give the earl the choice of securing it would be a service rendered him. If he were too poor to buy it, the thing would have to be considered."

"Nothing could make me touch money for it. George would never doubt we had concealed it in order to trick him out of it!"

"He will think so all the same. It will satisfy him, and not a

179

few besides, that Dawtie ought to have been convicted. The thing is certainly Mr. Crawford's—that is, his rather than yours. Your father undoubtedly meant him to have the cup, and God would not have you even to serve the right by taking advantage of an accident. Whatever ought to be done with the cup, Mr. Crawford ought to do it; it is his business to do right in regard to it; and whatever advantage may be gained by doing right, Mr. Crawford ought to have the chance of gaining it. Would you deprive him of the opportunity, to which at least he has a right, of doing justice, and delivering his soul?"

"You would have us tell the earl that his cup is found, but Mr. Crawford claims it?" said Alexa.

"An'rew would have us take it to Mr. Crawford," said Dawtie, "and tell him that the earl has a claim to it."

"Tell him also," said Andrew, "where it was found, showing he has no *legal* right to it; and tell him he had no more right to it than the laird could give him. Tell him, ma'am," continued Andrew, "that you expect him to take it to the earl who may buy it if he will—and say that if, after a fortnight, you find it is not in the earl's possession, you will yourself ascertain from the earl whether the offer has been made him."

"That is just right," said Alexa.

And so the thing was done. The cup soon came into the earl's collection, and without any further interference on her part.

A few days after she and Dawtie carried the cup to Crawford, a parcel arrived at Potlurg, containing a beautiful silver case, and inside the case the jeweled watch—with a letter from George begging Alexa to accept his present, and assuring her of his conviction that the moment he annoyed her with any further petition, she would return it. He expressed his regret that he had brought such suffering upon Dawtie, and said he was ready to make whatever amends her husband might think fit.

Alexa accepted the watch and wore it, for she thought her father would like her to do so.

Chapter 37.

THE FINAL SECRETS

The friendship of the three was never broken in all the many long years after that.

It was not true that, as she lay awake in the dark, the eyes of Alexa never renewed the tears of that autumn night on which she turned her back upon the pride of self; but her tears were never those of bitterness, of self-scorn, or of self-pity.

"If I am to be pitied," she would say to herself, "let the Lord pity me! I am not ashamed, and will not be sorry. I have nothing to resent, for no one has wronged me."

The three lived and worked and worshiped and grew side by side for many years, until Andrew died in middle age. His wife said the Master wanted him for something nobody else could do, or He would not have taken him from her. She wept and took comfort, for she lived in expectation.

One night, about a month after Andrew's burial, when Dawtie and Alexa were sitting together at Potlurg speaking of many things with the freedom of a long and tried love, Alexa asked, "Were you not very angry with me then, Dawtie?"

"When, ma'am?"

"When Andrew told you."

"Told me what, ma'am? I must be stupid tonight, for I canna think what you mean!"

"When he told you I wanted him, not knowing he was yours."

"I dinna know what ye're hinting at, ma'am!" persisted Dawtie, in a tone of bewilderment.

181

"Oh! I thought you had no secrets from one another!"

"I dinna know that we ever had—except things in his books that he said were God's secrets, which I should understand someday, for God was telling them as fast as He could to get His children to understand them."

"I see!" sighed Alexa. "You were made for each other! But this is my secret, and I have the right to tell it. He kept it for me to tell you, though I thought all the time you knew it!"

"I dinna want to know anything An'rew wouldna tell me."

"He thought it was my secret, you see, not his, and that was why he did not tell you."

"Of course, ma'am! An'rew always did what was right!"

"Well, Dawtie—I offered to be his wife if he would have me!"

"And what did he say?" asked Dawtie, with the composure of one listening to a story learned from a book.

"He told me he couldn't. But I'm not sure what he said. The words went away."

"When was it you asked him?" said Dawtie, sunk in thought.

"The night but one before the trial," answered Alexa.

"He might have taken you, then, instead of me! A lady and all! O ma'am! Do you think he took me 'cause I was in trouble? He might have been laird himself!"

"Dawtie! Dawtie!" cried Alexa. "If you think that would have weighed with Andrew, *I* ought to have been his wife, for I would have known him better than you!"

Dawtie smiled at that. "But I do know, ma'am," she said, "that An'rew was fit to cast the lairdship from him to comfort any poor lassie! I would have loved him all the same!"

"As I have done, Dawtie!" said Alexa solemnly. "But he wouldn't have thrown *me* away for you, if he hadn't loved you, Dawtie! Be sure of that. He might have made nothing of the lairdship, but he wouldn't have made nothing of me!"

"That's true, ma'am. I dinna doubt it."

"I love him still—and you mustn't mind me saying it, Dawtie! There are ways of loving that are good, though there be some pain in them."

Some thought Alexa hard, and some thought her cold, but the few that knew her, knew she was neither. And some will grant that such a friend as Andrew was better than such a husband as George.

182

Editor's Afterword.

Is this a happy ending? The answer depends upon your viewpoint. In a conventional ending, Andrew and Dawtie would live together happily ever after, Alexa would be provided a worthy husband—perhaps Sandy—in the course of later events, and the book would end before death or disaster came calling.

But MacDonald had the freedom and the desire to show that death is not the disaster we too often deem it to be, and that it does not have the power to override a conventional happy ending with the sadness that is also despair because it is without hope.

Sometimes his heroes and heroines die, to emphasize that for the believer, the only permanently happy life is the life forever that follows this one. In other books, as in *The Princess and Curdie*, MacDonald reminds us that righteousness and the fruits of righteousness are sought, achieved, and bestowed, but never inherited; that any earthly kingdom of whatever magnitude will pass away if it does not continue under holy princes and principles, and follow God in active obedience.

But in *The Elect Lady*, he shows that neither earthly happiness nor earthly suffering are everlasting. Earthly happiness may be swallowed up by earthly suffering, yet earthly suffering may itself be swallowed up by the unearthly peace that descends only from above and does not rise by itself in the human heart. Dawtie's love was not rooted in this world but in the next, for there both the source of her love and the object of her love were as well, and she was content to wait to see Andrew's face again, until she should see him side by side with her Saviour.

The ending may also reflect the personal lessons MacDonald had been learning at the cost of earthly grief; his father, his beloved brother, his half-sister, and three of his own children had all died before this book was written. He sorrowed, but with a heavenly sorrow, which seeks first and last its solace in the heart of the Father.

There may be another ending buried within the book—one taken from the many possibilities of life. All of MacDonald's novels are autobiographical in some of the events and personalities, if not in the actual story line. A self-confessed lover of both fine books and bright jewels, he perhaps saw the laird as the scarcely human and far from godly *thing* he would have become himself, had not God intervened and revealed to him the greater worth of the treasures that are laid up only in the world to come.

And among these mysteries, MacDonald leaves us wondering at the undefined meaning of his chosen title. Just who was the elect lady? Alexa, who at first thought herself to be one of the elect by birth and breeding and religious opinions? The church that met on the hillside with two boys, a girl, and a chicken? Or Dawtie, as the girl who was lifted up because she felt herself nothing in the eyes of Andrew?

Perhaps he meant us to think each possibility in its turn, in order that he might invert our thinking and bring Dawtie—at last—to the forefront, that we might consider one of the laws of the coming kingdom: the last shall be first, and those who humble themselves shall be exalted.

Notes, Quotes, and References.

1. Psyche and ego. The psyche is the soul (or spiritual part of man) in Greek philosophy, while the ego is that part of man which regards himself, or his personality.

2. Shadrach, Meshach, and Abednego. As related in Daniel 3, these three young men of God had defied the orders of Nebuchadnezzar to bow down to a golden idol, and so were condemned to die by being cast into a fiery furnace. However, they did not die, but were joined in the flames of the furnace by a fourth—Jesus Himself. The three emerged intact and unsinged, and their deliverance caused Nebuchadnezzar to bless God and grant men the freedom to worship Him.

3. A cottar-pair was a peasant who occupies a bit of ground leased from a tenant. The tenants leased their land from the laird, who owned it.

4. Rule of Three is the mathematic rule for determining the fourth term of a proportion where only three are known.

5. "My Nanie's Awa" is a song by Robert Burns (1759-1796), sung to the tune, "There'll never be peace till Jamie comes hame."

Now in her green mantle blythe Nature arrays,
And listens the lambkins that bleat o'er her braes;
While birds warble welcome in ilka green shaw,
But to me it's delightless—my Nanie's awa.

The snawdrap and primrose our woodlands adorn,
And violets bathe in the weet o' the morn;
They pain my sad bosom, sae sweetly they blaw,
They mind me o' Nanie—and Nanie's awa.

Thou lav'rock that springs frae the dews of the lawn,
The shepherd to warn o' the grey-breaking dawn,
And thou mellow mavis that hails the night-fa',
Give over for pity—my Nanie's awa.

Come Autumn, sae pensive, in yellow and grey,
And soothe me wi' tidings o' Nature's decay:
The dark, dreary Winter, and wild-driving snaw
Alane can delight me—now Nanie's awa.

6. Sonnet—by John Milton (1608-1674)

Lady, that in the prime of earliest youth,
    Wisely hast shun'd the broad way and the green,
    And with those few art eminently seen,
    That labour up the Hill of heav'nly Truth,
The better part with *Mary* and with *Ruth*,
    Chosen thou hast, and they that overween,
    And at thy growing vertues fret the spleen,
    No anger find in thee, but pity and ruth.
Thy care is fixt and zealously attends
    To fill thy odorous Lamp with deeds of light,
    And Hope that reaps not shame. Therefore be sure
Thou, when the Bridegroom with his feastfull friends
    Passes to bliss at the mid hour of night,
    Hast gain'd thy entrance, Virgin wise and pure.

7. Hinny, meaning "honey," is a term of affection.

8. "Bright shoots of everlastingness" and "Father of lights!

186

what sunny seed" are from poems by Henry Vaughan (1621-1695) in his *Silex Scintillans*.

"Bright shoots of everlastingness" is from the section entitled *The Retreat*.

Happy those early dayes! when I
Shin'd in my angel-infancy.
Before I understood this place
Appointed for my second race,
Or taught my soul to fancy aught
But a white, celestial thought,
When yet I had not walked above
A mile or two from my first love,
And looking back—at that short space—
Could see a glimpse of His bright face;
When on some gilded Cloud or flower
My gazing soul would dwell an hour,
And in those weaker glories spy
Some shadows of eternity;
Before I taught my tongue to wound
My Conscience with a sinful sound
Or had the black art to dispense
A sev'ral sin to ev'ry sence,
But felt through all this fleshly dress
Bright shoots of everlastingness.

O how I long to travel back
And tread again that ancient track!
That I might once more reach that plain,
Where first I left my glorious train;
From whence th' enlightened spirit sees
The shady City of palm trees.
But (ah!) my soul with too much stay
Is drunk, and staggers in the way.
Some men a forward motion love,
But I by backward steps would move,
And when this dust falls to the urn
In that state I came, return.

"Father of lights! what sunny seed" is from *Cock-Crowing*.

Father of lights! what sunny seed,
What glance of day hast Thou confin'd
Into this bird? To all the breed
This busie ray Thou hast assign'd;
    Their magnetism works all night,
    And dreams of Paradise and light.

Their eyes watch for the morning-hue,
Their little grain expelling night
So shines and sings, as if it knew
The path unto the house of light.
    It seems their candle, howe'r done,
    Was tinn'd and lighted at the sun.

If such a tincture, such a touch,
So firm a longing can impower,
Shall Thy own image think it much
To watch for Thy appearing hour?
    If a meer blast so fill the sail,
    Shall not the breath of God prevail?

O thou immortal light and heat!
Whose hand so shines through all this frame,
That by the beauty of the seat,
We plainly see, who made the same.
    Seeing thy seed abides in me,
    Dwell Thou in it, and I in Thee.

To sleep without Thee is to die;
Yea, 'tis a death partakes of hell;
For where Thou dost not close the eye,
it never opens, I can tell.
    In such a dark, Egyptian border,
    The shades of death dwell and disorder.

If joys and hopes and earnest throws
And hearts, whose Pulse beats still for light
Are given to birds; who, but Thee, knows
A lovesick soul's exalted flight?
    Can souls be track'd by any eye

But His, who gave them wings to flie?

Only this Veil which Thou hast broke,
And must be broken yet in me,
This veil, I say, is all the cloke
And cloud which shadows Thee from me.
　　This veil thy full-ey'd love denies,
　　And only gleams and fractions spies.

O take it off! make no delay,
But brush me with Thy light, that I
May shine into a perfect day,
And warm me at Thy glorious Eye!
　　O take it off! or till it flee,
　　Though with no Lilie, stay with me!

9. Satan is a leading character in John Milton's *Paradise Lost*.

10. Beatrice is the central character and spiritual guide in *The Divine Comedy (The Inferno, The Purgatorio, The Paradiso)* by Dante Alighieri (1265-1321).

11. Benvenuto Cellini (1500-1571) was an Italian goldsmith, artist, sculptor, and author. Some of his breathtakingly beautiful works have survived and may be seen in art museums. One of his patrons was Pope Clement VII.

12. Clement the Seventh (1475-1534) was Pope from 1523-1534. His reign was marked by war and by Henry VIII's revolt against the Roman Catholic Church. He was a patron not only of Cellini, but also of Raphael and Michelangelo.

13. Cardinal York (Henry Benedict Stuart, 1725-1807) was the brother of Charles Edward Stuart, "The Young Pretender."

14. Charles Edward Stuart (1720-1788) was the beloved "Bonnie Prince Charlie" and "The Young Pretender" of Scottish history. He led the Jacobite uprising, whose hopes were ultimately crushed at Culloden Moor in 1746.

15. The Duchess of Albany (1752-1824) was the wife of Charles Edward Stuart, from their marriage in 1772 until their separation eight years later.

16. A casuist is one who attempts to appease his conscience by rationalization and the application of general ethical principles to specific questions of duty.

17. Louis Elzevir (1540-1617) was a Dutch publisher who printed inexpensive but good books, prized first by impoverished scholars and later by book collectors. The books printed by him and his descendants are often referred to as *Elzevirs*.

18. "Lease were out." The laird leased parcels of his land to the tenants. If the laird desired to be rid of troublesome tenants, he could simply refuse to renew their leases, or make the terms of renewal too stiff to be affordable. Those tenants would then have to leave their holdings and make new leases elsewhere.

19. The gloaming is the profoundly beautiful and peaceful Scottish twilight. The quality and effects of this richly colored sunset and its aftermath cannot easily be described in words, and are best known only by those who have experienced it. The gloaming is frequently linked to romantic or momentous events in Scottish literature.

20. Enoch was the only man, other than Elijah, to be taken directly from this life into God's presence without tasting death. (Genesis 5:18-24; Hebrews 11:5)

21. A cheapjack is a dealer in inferior or worthless merchandise.

22. Madame de Genlis (1746-1830) was a French writer and royal governess.

23. Ninon de Lenclos (1620-1705) was a French courtesan and philosopher. Her intellectual admirers included the playwright Moliere and the poet Paul Scarron. Paul Scarron's

widow, in her later role as Madame de Maintenon, was a benefactor of de Lenclos. She left money in her will to buy books for the young Voltaire.

24. Madame de Maintenon (1635-1717) was the second wife (and untitled queen) of Louis XIV, King of France.

25. Dr. Faustus was, by legend, a sixteenth-century German doctor who sold his soul to the devil in exchange for knowledge, youth, and magical power. Christopher Marlowe and Goethe had both dramatized and popularized the legend in writing by MacDonald's time. Several musical works had also been based upon the story, including the ballad referred to here.

26. The Holy Grail is also known as the Sangreal. According to medieval legend, the Grail is the cup that was (1) used by Christ for the celebration of the Last Supper, (2) used by Joseph of Arimathea to catch the blood from the crucified Christ's side, (3) brought to England by Joseph. A vision of the Grail would be revealed to only the holiest and purest of knights; it is so treated in the legends of King Arthur and his court.

27. Assizes were court sessions held on a periodic basis. Many rural districts had no permanent magistrate, and could conduct their court business only when a traveling magistrate came to town to hold the assizes.

28. A yowie is a young female sheep; the word was also an affectionate term of endearment for a girl.

29. "Not Proven" is a court verdict which proclaims that while the defendant may indeed be guilty, he has not been proven guilty by the evidence. Such a verdict tends to cast a shadow of doubt over the defendant's character for the rest of his life.

30. An Arminian is a person who follows the teachings of Arminius. This theology opposes Calvin's absolute determinism

and maintains a real possibility of salvation for all men.

31. A Socinian is a person who follows the teachings of Faustus Socinus. This theology denies the Trinity and eternal punishment.

32. A Swedenborgian is a person who follows the teachings of Emanuel Swedenborg. This theology proclaims a new dispensation, teaches direct contact with the spiritual world, and interprets Scripture in a spiritual or symbolic manner.

33. An Arian is a person who follows the teachings of Arius. Arius taught that God was separate and unknowable, and that Christ was created and neither truly God nor truly man. His doctrine was condemned at the Councils of Nicaea (A.D. 325) and Constantinople (A.D. 381).